It was so cool the way this was working out. She never would have dreamed what kind of miracles God would work when she had offered her simple prayer to sell her cookies.

"Hey, Erin . . . ," she started, wanting to share the joy with her sis. But her voice drifted off to nothing as she remembered their fight. Erin didn't turn around. Tess felt her stomach drop to the bottom of a well. The money wouldn't mean anything if she lost Erin.

Secret Sisters: (se'-krit sis'-terz) n. Two friends who choose each other to be everything a real sister should be: loyal and loving. They share with and help each other no matter what!

Secret ✳ *Sisters*

Accidental Angel

Sandra Byrd

WATERBROOK
PRESS
COLORADO SPRINGS

ACCIDENTAL ANGEL

PUBLISHED BY WATERBROOK PRESS

5446 North Academy Boulevard, Suite 200

Colorado Springs, Colorado 80918

A division of Bantam Doubleday Dell Publishing Group, Inc.

Scriptures in the Secret Sisters series are quoted from the
International Children's Bible, New Century Version,
© 1986, 1988 by Word Publishing,
Dallas, Texas 75039. Used by permission.

ISBN 1-57856-018-7

1998—First Edition

1 3 5 7 9 10 8 6 4 2

For Les and Grace Byrd,
who gave me their Christmas angel
as well as their love.

one

Don't Look Now

Tuesday, December 17

"Quick! Help me with the box before it drops." Tess Thomas wrestled with a huge carton of Christmas lights.

Her best friend and Secret Sister, Erin Janssen, set down her can of soda and ran to help Tess. "Wow! How many strands are in there?" Erin asked, peering into the open box after they set it down.

"Six hundred and forty-nine." Tess giggled as she brushed her coarse brown hair back from her sweaty forehead. "Just kidding! All I know is that we have to have them all strung up and blinking in an hour so we're ready to go when my mom comes." Lots of activity bustled around the girls—people unpacking cartons and setting up decorations for the Community Center's annual Christmas craft fair.

"It was so cool of Katie and Joann to invite us." Erin wound a long string of blinking chili-pepper lights around her elbow and hand. Katie Hernandez and Joann Waters were two girls in Tess and Erin's sixth-grade class.

"I know. I'm glad we shared our secret with them last month on the field trip to the planetarium. Now they can be Secret Sisters to each other, just like you and me!" Tess plugged in one of the already untangled sets.

Then the girls worked to sort more lights. Both of them had only brothers, but they really wanted a sister. So, they chose each other to be a sister, in secret. They were best buds and closer than lots of real sisters. But they didn't tell everyone.

"Now we have a Secret Sisters booth—you and me as sister team number one, and Katie and Joann as sister team number two." Tess smiled. Katie had invited them to share their booth at the craft fair. Her mom, Mrs. Hernandez, was in charge.

"Did you pack all our placemats in a box so they'll be ready to go Saturday morning?" Tess asked as she tested another set of lights.

"Yes," Erin answered. "I think there are a hundred. If we sell them for a dollar a piece, we should each have fifty dollars after the show."

"That fifty dollars will really help pay the way toward horse camp this summer," Tess said. "I'm so excited I can barely wait another six months! But I know my parents won't have a lot of extra money, with the new baby coming and all."

"Well, our placemats turned out really pretty. And since we used up all the cards my mom had left over from her job"—Mrs. Janssen stocked greeting cards at drugstores and grocery stores—"we didn't have to pay much for materials. Which leaves more money for camp!" Erin said with a smile.

Over the last week the two of them had carefully cut off the greeting card covers and laid them out in a place-mat pattern, then covered them top and bottom with clear plastic contact paper. No two were alike, but each was festive. Some had saguaro cacti strung with silver tinsel and tiny white lights. Some featured rodeo set-tings to celebrate the Arizona-style Christmas both girls had always known. A few were more traditional, with snowy pines seemingly dipped in powdered sugar. It had taken hours to complete them. Pretty and inexpen-sive, the mats would sell quickly—at least the girls hoped so.

"That is so cool! This will be the first year I have enough money to buy some really nice presents," Tess answered. "Usually I end up buying something cheesy, like salt and pepper shakers. But this year will be differ-ent. I want to celebrate Christmas in a special way." Candy stripes shone on her face as she wound red-and-white strands of lights around a four-foot-high plastic cane. Mrs. Hernandez walked up and winked apprecia-tively.

"You girls are doing a fine job. And it's wonderful of you to offer to help us set up. There's more to planning a craft fair than most people realize." A lovely smile creased her soft brown face as she patted Erin on the back. "Just make sure all the chili-pepper lights are strung by the entrance." She pointed at the door where all guests and customers would enter the show. "I don't know if Katie and Joann told you, but when I checked with Mrs. Austin, she said you had booth number one. Right inside the door—a high-traffic area."

"That is so great!" Tess said. "Thanks. Can we go see it?"

"Sure." Mrs. Hernandez smiled at Tess's enthusiasm. "Just make sure the lights get done." With that she scurried over to supervise the snack area construction.

Tess and Erin set aside their lights and hurried to check out their booth. "Can you believe it? What a great spot!" Erin marveled. "We're going to sell all our placemats for sure."

After plotting how they would lay out the placemat display, along with the painted plant pots Katie and Joann had made, they returned to the lights to finish their task.

"What are you guys going to do for Christmas?" Erin asked, passing the time.

"Well, since we're staying home this year, we'll probably have French toast fondue, like we always do, then open presents on Christmas day. I don't know. What about you guys?"

"We open presents on Christmas morning and go to church on Christmas Eve. Are you going to come to church?" Erin asked.

"Um, I don't know. I'd really like to, but I haven't asked my parents. I think I might feel weird on Christmas without them. It's not like Sunday school, you know." Tess didn't look up as she talked. She had become a Christian in October and usually went to church with Erin's family. It wasn't too strange to go without her parents because she was just in Sunday school with the other sixth graders. But on Christmas Day there was no Sunday school. Instead, everyone was in the service. With their families. And since her parents weren't Christians, she didn't think they would want to go.

"Didn't you tell me they went to church on Christmas at your grandparents' in Minnesota?" Erin said.

"Yes," Tess answered. "But that's only because we were guests. We've never gone when it's just been our family at home."

"Well, there's a Christmas Eve service, too, if they would rather go then. But whatever they decide, you can always come with us. Just let me know."

They went back to replacing bulbs and stringing, with Erin unraveling and Tess moving from one step on the ladder to the next, winding the lights on the nails already in place from last year's fair. She saved the chili-pepper lights for last and set the ladder by the front door to begin hanging them. As she peered out the door, she saw a familiar van pull into the parking lot. *Oh-oh.* Tess's heart sank like a quarter to the bottom of a pool. It was Colleen's van.

Colleen Clark was Tess's best friend last summer, or so Tess had thought. When it came time to start sixth grade, though, Colleen turned out to be two-faced, letting her best friend from fifth grade, Lauren, boss her around. When Tess refused to pick on another girl as an initiation rite into Colleen and Lauren's Coronado Club, they had humiliated Tess instead. She knew they were planning to be at the craft fair but kept hoping they would change their minds. It seemed they hadn't.

"Hey!" Tess climbed down the ladder and waved to Erin, who was handing the now-empty light box to Mrs. Hernandez.

Erin hurried over. "What's up?"

"Don't look now, but guess who is coming. The Coronado Club." Tess pointed to Lauren, Colleen, and Melody, who strode in long, confident steps toward the community center.

"Blow them off. Who cares?" Erin said. They ducked inside their booth, under the temporary sign that read "Booth #1."

Colleen came in first, flipping back her shiny hair. She surveyed the room as if she were the building's owner. Melody, the cutest girl in the sixth grade, trailed behind, pursing her bow-shaped lips so that her dimples stood out to their best advantage. Last, but certainly not least, came Lauren. She hooked her thumbs into her jeans' belt loops and stood square in front of Tess and Erin.

"Well, it looks as if someone's hanging out in our booth. Sorry, girls, but you'll have to leave. We paid for booth one, and it's ours. Take off!"

two

Sore Losers,
Sore Winners

Tuesday, December 17

"There must be a mistake," Tess countered, trying to keep her temper—and her fear—under control. "Mrs. Hernandez just told us this was our booth."

"Read this." Lauren fished a postcard out of her backpack.

She flipped it toward Erin, who took it from her and read, "Confirmation of booth registration, Booth #1. Please bring final payment on Tuesday, December 17."

"And here's the final payment. Let's go find Mrs. Hernandez."

Tess and Erin tagged along behind the Coronado Club as they went over to find Katie's mother and sort things out.

"Ugh," Mrs. Hernandez grunted as she stood up from rolling a plastic runner over the low carpet to protect it from heavy foot traffic. "What's up, girls?"

"Apparently someone made a mistake. We paid for

booth number one. Here's the rest of our money."
Lauren thrust a check at Mrs. Hernandez. "But these
two think the booth is theirs. Maybe you can straighten
them out." Lauren huffed angrily, but Melody still
smiled her Shirley Temple smile. Colleen just looked at
her shoes.

"Let's see." Mrs. Hernandez took the card and looked
it over. After a minute she turned to Erin and Tess. "I'm
afraid she's right, girls. We've made a mistake. We'll
have to let them have first priority. They paid for their
booth, but yours is complimentary."

"See!" Lauren looked at Tess and Erin. "Get your stuff
out of there."

"We didn't put anything in there, so don't get your
undies in a bundle!" Tess answered.

"Tess." Erin whispered a warning.

Tess nodded. *Cool down*, she thought to herself as the
Coronado Club headed back toward their booth.

"Where should we go then?" Tess asked Mrs. Hernandez.

"Well, unfortunately, the last time I checked only two
booths were left, toward the back. It's not easily acces-
sible, but it's all we have left. Why don't you girls go
over and see whether you prefer number thirty-five or
thirty-six."

"Okay," Erin sighed. They walked toward the back of
the room, looking at the booth numbers as they passed.
"This makes me so mad! They always get their way.
First in school and now this!"

"I know," Tess agreed. "It's so unfair. It's like if you're popular, everything goes your way. Thanks for reminding me not to lose my temper though. I don't want them to think we're sore losers. We already know they're sore winners."

Finally the girls found the remaining booths—way, way in the back. Booth thirty-five was tucked into a corner, easy to pass right by it. Booth thirty-six wasn't much better, but at least it stuck out a bit.

"Yuck. Nobody but the janitors will come back this far. Now what?" Erin asked.

"I don't know." Tess answered glumly. "I guess we better tell her to save booth thirty-six for us."

Erin said, "I'm sure Joann and Katie will agree."

After checking with Mrs. Austin, Katie's mother assured the girls that booth thirty-six would be saved for them and that she would tell Katie and Joann that night.

"Come on, my mom is going to be here in a minute." Tess picked up her backpack, and she and Erin headed out into the twilight.

Night birds gently called to one another, almost whispering in and among the orange trees. Perching on skinny limbs with glossy green leaves, the birds took refuge in the perfumed desert evening.

"Isn't it a nice night?" Erin asked, turning her head to allow the mild breezes of winter in Scottsdale, Arizona, to swirl around her head. The girls wore long-sleeved shirts, but no outer covering was necessary. Erin pulled the French braid out of her hair, and it fell in long, golden kinks to her shoulders. Car lights approached, and she asked, "Is that your mom?"

A Jeep raced up the street and skidded to a noisy stop just in front of the community center, stubbing one front tire on the curb. Tess cringed. "Yes," she said, turning red from fingertips to forehead. Molly Thomas, Tess's mother, was a notoriously bad driver. Not unsafe, just clumsy.

"Hi Mom." Tess climbed in and kissed her mother on the cheek. "How was your day?"

"Busy. I had a deadline and barely made it. Express mailed it just before I picked you guys up." Tess's mother wrote advertising copy, the words used in ads to sell things, for a Los Angeles advertising firm. Although her office was in their home, she still had deadlines to meet. "I need to stop at the store on the way to Erin's. We need some hamburger and tortillas for tacos tonight. I'm hungry."

"Eating for two, remember?" Tess reminded Erin as her mother patted her tummy. Mrs. Thomas was expecting a baby in late June.

"I don't have to be home for another half-hour or so," Erin said, checking her watch.

After Mrs. Thomas jammed the car into first gear, they were off. "Where's Tyler?" Tess asked. Usually her brother would have come along for the ride.

Tess picked a remnant of icy pink polish off her thumbnail. She had to remember to buy some green polish before Christmas.

"At Big Al's. We'll pick him up after we drop off Erin."

"Oh, great. I hope he doesn't bring home some disease."

"Now, Tess," her mother said, "you shouldn't tease Big Al like that. He's really a good friend for Tyler and a nice kid. Just a little different."

"Yeah, like from another galaxy."

"Here we are." Mrs. Thomas swung the midnight-blue Jeep into the parking lot and shut off the engine.

"I want to buy some nail polish. Can we meet you back at the registers?" Tess asked as they got out of the car.

"Yes, but don't take too long," her mother answered.

"I need some nail polish. And some lip gloss. Should we get new flavors, Erin?" Tess asked, walking toward the beauty supplies.

"Definitely. Mine's almost gone, and besides, it's a summer flavor. Let's see what else they have."

After uncapping and sniffing several flavors, Tess decided on Sugar Plum and Erin on Hot Chocolate. Tess found some Christmas-green nail paint, and they went toward the front of the store to make their purchases.

"Are your parents going to let you wear that green polish? I don't think mine would," Erin said.

"I don't know. But I really want to try it, so I'm going to buy it and see what they say."

Tess's mother brought her cart around to where the girls stood. "Hi there. All set?"

"Yep."

"Do you want me to buy your stuff?" Mrs. Thomas asked Tess.

"No, I'll do it." Tess wasn't ready to ask about the green polish quite yet.

"Okay," her mother said. "I'll go first, then I can get the car while you guys pay." Her mom paid for her purchases and went out to the parking lot.

"Hey, what's this?" Tess pointed to the pad of printed paper by the cashier.

"It's a Scan-Away Hunger form," the cashier answered.

"What's that?"

"You take one off and hand it to me with your purchases, and I charge you an extra $1.29, which goes to the rescue mission downtown to feed the homeless."

"Really? For only $1.29? That's cheaper than my lip gloss," Tess said. "I'll take one." The cashier rang up her purchases, and then Erin's. They walked outside and hopped into the waiting Jeep.

"Hey, Mom, I paid for a homeless person's meal," Tess told her.

"That's sweet, honey. You have such a tender heart. Did you guys have a fun time setting up the craft fair?"

"Well . . . ," Tess started.

"The Coronado Club took our booth," Erin finished.

"Oh, dear. How did that happen?" Mrs. Thomas said.

While the girls explained the situation, Tess's mother shook her head in dismay. "I hope you'll still be able to sell all your placemats even if the booth position isn't as nice," she commented.

"Me, too," Tess said. But her voice betrayed her doubt.

Later that night Tess logged into her computer diary.

Dear God,

Do you remember how much I wanted to go to horse camp with Erin this summer? I mean, I need to go this summer? Well, I asked for a deposit to the camp for Christmas, and I think I'm going to get it. But I still need to save up money to help pay the rest, plus I want to buy some really good presents this year. So my plan was to use the money from the craft fair. But now the Coronado Club practically snatched away our booth, and we're way back in dustball alley, as Grandma Kate always says. So how am I going to make the money? Thanks for listening.

Love, Tess

three

Gross Grilled Cheese

Wednesday, December 18

During class the next day, with only a week left before Christmas vacation, Tess doodled on her health book cover while Ms. Martinez lectured on the food pyramid. Ripping off a corner of the cover, Tess wrote on it, "Are you as bored as I am?" and passed it to Erin.

Erin formed the scrap into a ball and stuck it into her shoe, rolling her eyes at Tess and pretending to snore. Ms. M. was a good teacher, but even so, Tess wished recess would hurry up.

Finally, it arrived. Tess pulled on her jeans jacket, grabbed her snack, and walked outside with Erin. "Did you tell Katie and Joann about the booth?"

"No, I haven't talked with them. Let's go find them. Oh yeah, here." Erin handed Tess a girls' magazine. "Are you ready to switch yet?"

As Secret Sisters, Tess and Erin did lots of special things just between the two of them. Like sharing magazine subscriptions. They liked two magazines so they each subscribed to one and then, halfway through the month, they switched. That way they read two magazines for the price of one.

"Yeah, but I forgot my magazine. I'll bring it tomorrow. Okay, Sis?" Tess slid the magazine Erin handed her into her backpack to read that afternoon.

"Okay, Sis," Erin answered, and they clinked charm bracelets to seal the deal. Then they went in search of their friends. Katie and Joann hung out at the edge of the playground.

"Hey, guys, did you hear about our booth?" Erin asked.

"Yeah, bummer," Joann answered. Her glossy black cornrows glistened in the high winter sun. Tess fingered one.

"How do you get these cool beads in there?"

"Weaving. It's like braiding. It takes practice, and my aunt helps me. When I was little, I liked lots of beads because I liked the sound they made as they clanked together when I ran. But now I think just a few are prettier." Joann always dressed sharp and earned good grades. Sometimes she knew it all, which could be annoying, but as Tess got to know her better, she liked Joann more.

"I think they're pretty, too," Tess said.

"Hey," Katie said, "my mom wants to know what your craft is. You guys didn't register it with her yesterday, and since only one booth is allowed to sell each kind of craft, you need to let her know." When Katie Hernandez smiled, her plump cheeks tinged with pink and gently squeezed her happy brown eyes. "What are you guys making?"

"We already finished," Erin said proudly. "We made holiday placemats from old Christmas cards, covered in plastic. We saw the idea in one of my mom's magazines."

"Oh, that sounds cool. I haven't seen any of those before. They should sell," Katie concluded.

"We hope so," Tess said. "I'm already planning what to do with my money."

"What?" Katie asked, moving closer.

"Well, first I'm going to buy some presents for my mom, dad, and brother. Last year, when I didn't have any money, I bought some really cheesy presents. Then, best of all, Erin and I want to go to the Lazy K Bar Ranch for camp this summer. For Christmas we're asking our parents for the deposit to the camp, to guarantee us a spot this summer. But I need some cash to help pay for the rest. I'm sure my parents will chip in some, but not all of it."

"I forgot you guys like horses so much," Joann said. "That sounds totally fun. Do you think your parents will get you that for Christmas? My dad always says he likes to pick out my present so I'm surprised."

"Yeah, I'm sure they'll think it's okay," Tess replied, swallowing the last of her chocolate milk. "They already approved going to camp. Lazy K Bar has been around a long time. Erin's grandpa knows one of the wranglers. And my dad thinks sports are healthy."

"I already asked," Erin said. "So we'll see!"

"I'm buying presents, too. Then I want a telescope," Joann said.

"Oh wow, can I come over when you get it?" Tess

wanted to be some kind of scientist when she grew up. Maybe an astronomer.

"Sure. We'd better pack it up. Looks like everybody is heading in. Don't look now, but here come Kenny and Russell. Just seeing them gives me a migraine," Katie teased. Kenny and Russell were the class goof-ups, but ever since they had gotten in trouble last month for throwing rotten tomatoes off the bus, they had cooled down. "Don't forget to call my mom about your craft," she reminded Tess.

"I won't." Tess pushed her hair back as she pulled herself off the ground.

She glanced at the rusty clay mountains looming in the distance. No snow ever crowned their peaks, but they had a peculiar beauty. Their rocky edges and jagged peaks guarded Coronado Elementary School, reminding Tess how good it was to live in Arizona.

What wasn't good was being the oldest. Tess always had to be in charge, even if she didn't feel like it. That day, after school, she met Tyler and groaned when she saw that Big Al was with him.

"Didn't know they let you out of the zoo today," she said to Big Al.

"Yeah, well, I got a visitors' pass to come and see you," Al growled back. "Come on, Tyler, let's go." Together the threesome walked the few short blocks to the Thomases' house, and Tess unlocked the door.

A note waited for them on the refrigerator. "Please fix yourselves a snack. I've gone to the doctor, and I'll be back by 4:30. Love, Mom."

Great. In charge again. "I'm going to read my new magazine. Can you guys keep it down?" Tess asked.

"Righto," Tyler answered. He loved British mystery shows and often talked like his detective heroes. "We have a right top secret project anyway."

Tess dug in the cupboard for a snack and took the bait. "What kind of assignment?"

"An extremely important one," Big Al answered. "One we've been working on all year."

"Hey, ol' girl," Tyler said, "where's Mom's postal scale? You know, the one that weighs in ounces?"

"In her office," Tess answered. She sensed something tricky going on, something she might get in trouble for not preventing. "What are you two up to?"

"Hold that thought!" Tyler said, racing from the room and returning a minute later with the scale. He pulled a Kleenex from his pocket and dumped a pile of lint on the scale. "I say, three ounces! Jolly good. Let's see you beat that, old boy!"

In spite of herself, Tess was intrigued. Big Al pulled a plastic bag out of his pocket, also full of multicolored lint balls. Placing the balls on the scale he read, "Three and one-half ounces. I win!"

"Good show, ol' boy. But this is only the beginning. We measure again next month." Tyler laughed.

"What is that?" Tess asked, pointing to the collections of lint.

"Toe cheese," Big Al answered.

"What's that?"

"You know, when you take off your socks at night and

lint is between your toes? We've been saving it for months, to see who has the most. It's best right after school, when your feet are sweaty."

"That is so disgusting! I am never getting married if boys are all like this."

"I wouldn't worry," Big Al said. "Want a grilled toe cheese sandwich?"

"Blech. I'm leaving. Don't turn on the stove or anything. I'll be in the family room reading if you want me." Tess grabbed a cupcake, a glass of milk, and her magazine. She flopped down on the family room's carpeted floor and started to read.

"I hate all these insert cards," she muttered, ripping them out. "The magazine never stays open." She ripped out two or three and then stopped at the fourth. A round, angular face with liquid brown eyes stared at her. The card read, "Wouldn't you like to give this little one a Christmas she won't forget? Please send any donation, and we will purchase and deliver the gift to a needy child in Jesus' name." Tess couldn't take her eyes away from the girl, and remembering how good it felt to donate the Scan-Away meal, she decided to send in the card.

"I'll have plenty of money after the craft show," she told herself, filling in her name and address, writing "$5" on the amount line, and checking "bill me." As she stuffed the last piece of chocolate cupcake into her mouth and licked the frosting from her thumb and forefinger, she headed to the mailbox. It felt good to do something nice for a kid who had so little.

four

Christmas Angels

Wednesday Afternoon, December 18

After mailing the card and finishing her snack, Tess remembered Goldy. She headed past Tyler's room and down the hall to her own room. Goldy swam round and round in her bowl, which was perched on Tess's grandmother's old trunk. Tess tapped the glass she had cleaned only yesterday.

"How are you, girl?" she asked. Not knowing for sure if the fish was a girl or a boy, Tess always assumed the best, that Goldy was a girl. Shaking some fish flakes into the water, Tess then went to the kitchen and dialed the Hernandezes' number.

"Hi, Katie, can I talk with your mom?" She twirled her hair around her finger as she waited for Mrs. Hernandez.

"Mrs. Hernandez? This is Tess Thomas. I'm calling to register our craft. We're making placemats." Untwirling her hair while she waited for Mrs. Hernandez to give her an A-Okay, she suddenly stopped.

"I'm sorry, Tess, but someone has already registered placemats. The rules of the craft fair are that no booth can sell anything similar to another booth's craft. So you'll have to choose something else. I'm sorry. This doesn't seem to be going smoothly for you, does it?" Mrs. Hernandez sounded loving but firm. Like a mom.

"What do you mean, someone already made placemats? But ours are done! I mean, we've already made them! Is there . . . is there any chance of bending the rules?"

"I'm sorry. Do you have another idea?"

"I know we should have checked before we made them. We just forgot. Well, okay, um, I'll talk with Erin and call you back with another idea. Thank you. Bye."

Tess could barely hold back the tears until she hung up. All their hard work for nothing! They might as well throw away those dumb placemats. With the craft fair two days away and no money to buy materials, all her dreams of a merry Christmas were over. Worse yet, her best friend and Secret Sister might get a spot at camp while Tess wouldn't. Which meant that Erin would be going without Tess. And riding with someone else.

Just then she heard the electric garage door open, and she ran out the back to greet her mother. Mrs. Thomas had pulled the car into the garage and had just opened the car door when Tess pounced on her. "This is awful. It's the worst day of my life," she moaned.

"What, honey, what?" Mrs. Thomas put her arm around Tess's shoulder, and they walked into the house.

"Someone else is already making placemats for the craft fair. So we can't sell ours, and we have hardly any time and no money. First our booth is stolen by the Coronado Club. Then our placemats are down the drain. It's so unfair. What can we do?"

"Well, I don't know. Let's sit down for a minute and pull our thoughts together. Hmm." Tess's mother sat on the family room sofa with her feet curled beneath her. "Where's Tyler? What's that mess on the floor?" She gestured at the ripped-out cards.

"Oh, Tyler and Big Al are in Tyler's room measuring toe cheese," Tess said. When her mother raised her eyebrows in question, Tess added, "Don't ask. And those are cards I ripped out of my magazine. I sent one in to the Christmas Angel Foundation to give a gift to a poor kid for Christmas." Tess wrinkled her brow. "Maybe I should go pull it out of the mail. Now that I'll have no money, that is."

"You're too late. The mail carrier came just as I pulled in. Now, let's put our heads together and think of what else you can do." Tess lay on the floor, feet propped up next to her mother on the couch. Frustrated thoughts elbowed each other in her mind. She shouldn't have sent in that card before making the money. Although she did have a little baby-sitting money saved. But now that would have to go to the Christmas presents. A minute later she rolled over and sat up.

"I have it!"

"What?" her mother said.

"Christmas angels. The name of that program reminded me of those Christmas angel cookies you and Grandma Kate make. You know, with the melted hard candy inside their wings so they look like stained glass? Those always look great, and they are totally tasty. Would you help us?"

"Sure," her mother said. "But you're going to have to make a lot of cookies. Why don't you call Erin and see if it's okay with her. Maybe she and her mother could come over to bake Friday night. Then check in with Mrs. Hernandez to make sure no one else is making something similar."

"Okay! I'll be right back." Tess ran to use the phone in her room as she saw her mother head toward the kitchen to start dinner.

A minute later Tess was in her room, dialing like crazy. "Hello, Erin? Bad news and good news. Which do you want first?"

"Bad news," Erin answered across the line. "Might as well get it over with."

"Bad news is we can't sell our placemats."

"What are you talking about? Why not?"

" 'Cause I called Katie's mom, and she said someone else was already doing them."

"You are kidding! What a bummer! Well, what are we going to do then? And what are we going to do with all those placemats?"

"I don't know about the placemats, but I have a really good idea. We can make Christmas angel cookies. My mom has a great recipe. The cookies are like sugar cookies, but you cut them with angel cookie cutters. Then, you melt hard candies in holes you cut out so that they look like stained glass. You and your mom could come over and bake with us on Friday night so they would be fresh Saturday. We could decorate our booth with those little angel dolls of your mom's, if she would let us borrow them. What do you think?"

"Well, I'm sad about the placemats. I mean, we worked really hard on them. I suppose we could each take some for our own Christmas dinners. Hmm. I guess the cookies sound like a good idea. I'll check with my mom and call you back if there's a problem. Did you call Katie's mom to make sure the cookies are okay?"

"No, but I'll do that. Do you, um, think Tom could come and help us set up our booth?" Tess blushed a bit as she said it.

"I'll ask your Romeo. Okay, Juliet?" Erin teased. Tom was Erin's blond brother, two years older than Tess and Erin. Tess thought he was great. She didn't know if he was really a Romeo, but maybe close. He definitely didn't save his toe cheese.

"Okay, see you tomorrow, Sis," Tess said. After hanging up she dialed Mrs. Hernandez, then went back into the kitchen.

"Great news, Mom. Mrs. Hernandez said angel cookies are fine. Someone is selling dip and soup mixes but no cookies. We're set."

"Set for what?" Tyler strode into the room.

"For my craft fair. Where's Big Al?" Tess asked.

"His brother just came to get him. They walked home. Say, is that the craft fair I am going to?"

"No, I think not."

"Well, Tess . . . ," her mom said.

"No way, Mom. He's not coming. I can't have him there. I'd rather shave my head and be bald than take him."

"I've been meaning to tell you. Dad and I have an appointment at the bank on Saturday morning. I tried to change it, but I couldn't. And Saturday is the only day Dad can go. So Tyler will have to go with you, but just for a couple of hours."

"All right! I can sell my Cricket Lickets!" Tyler jumped into the air.

"Mom, he can't come! Why do I always have to be in charge of him? It's not my fault I'm the oldest. Is this just going to get worse when the baby is born?" Tess huffed and turned toward her brother. "And I don't care what you think you are going to sell. Those cricket lollipops will make everybody so sick to their stomachs they won't want to buy my cookies! You can't talk to anyone. Nobody."

"Do you think I want to talk to your goofy friends? I'd rather be tortured by space aliens."

"Mom," Tess pleaded, "it's so babyish to have my little brother there. Do you guys think I'm a little kid?"

"No, I am well aware that you'll be twelve next month. In fact, I've planned something special for your birthday. But you need to work together with the family. We all have responsibilities, and part of yours is caring for Tyler. He's going, or you can stay home."

Tess could see that her mother meant it. Nodding silent agreement, Tess walked toward her room. Just great. Wait till the Coronado Club got a view of Tyler manning the booth with them. How uncool.

five

Christmas Lost

Thursday Evening, December 19

"Where's the list?" Tess's mother placed a ten-pound bag of flour in their cart, then waited while Tess unfolded the notebook paper she had shoved into her pocket.

"Here. We need sugar, vanilla, and some lemon extract. Also all the hard candies. I don't see any though."

"We won't find them in the baking aisle. After we finish here, we'll head over to the candy row. I need to buy extra hard candies for Tyler to melt down for his homemade lollipops, too."

The store was crowded tonight. Everyone seemed to be stocking up on last-minute items for Christmas baking. Grandma Kate usually baked with Tess and her mom, but this year she was visiting Tess's uncle instead.

"How many cookies do you think we should make? I mean, we still want to earn about a hundred dollars. Of course, I don't know what we'll do with the cookies if they don't sell." Tess hesitated. She hadn't thought about not selling them all, but it was a distinct possibility since their booth was so out of the way.

"I'd sell them two for a dollar. They are pretty big and a lot of work goes into making the melted candies look like stained glass." Her mother lifted a sack of sugar from the shelf, brushing off some loose granules from a broken package alongside the one she chose.

"That means we have to make two hundred cookies!" Tess grabbed a pen from her mom's purse and quickly divided by twelve. "That's sixteen dozen!"

"Not including broken ones, which there are sure to be a few. Or ones snitched for snacking," her mom reminded her.

"Well, I hope we can do it. I already have plans for the money!" Tess said.

"Just make sure those plans include sharing the cost of ingredients with me. I'll pay for them now, but I'll want half of what the cost is back after the fair." Mrs. Thomas steered the cart out of the baking aisle and over to the candy row. At Christmastime an entire row was devoted to sweets, not only red-and-white-striped canes but also dark chocolate trees and hard candy ribbons folded over like expensive hair bows in pink and teal and yellow. Tiny snowballs of dates rolled in coconut shone from beneath plastic. Finally Tess spotted the hard candy—glistening rubies, sapphires, and emeralds in twisted clear wrappers.

"How many bags do we need?"

"I'm not sure," her mother answered. "This is the first

time I've done this without Grandma Kate. Let's buy four bags."

Tess grabbed the candy bags and set them in the cart. "Don't forget the lights. And the cider," she reminded her mother.

"Right. We need two indoor strings, which we'll put on the tree tonight, and two outdoor strings, which Dad and Tyler can put up."

"I hope they picked out a good tree. Last year Tyler picked one that had a big hole on one side, and we couldn't hang any ornaments over it," Tess said.

"I'm sure it'll be okay. We'll just turn any bad spots to face the wall."

Because the trees had to come from far away, like Oregon and Washington, they didn't last very long before the evergreens dried out. But still Tess hoped they wouldn't encounter any decorating challenges because of problems with the tree.

"I think that's it. Let's check out and go home to see what kind of tree they found."

A half-hour later Tess lugged the last grocery bag into the kitchen just as her dad and Tyler pulled into the driveway. "Did you get one? Did you get a good one?" she asked, running out to examine the pine roped to the Jeep's roof.

"Yes, we found a good one." Mr. Thomas patted her on the shoulder, then reached up to untie the tree. "Can you hold it steady while I loosen this?" he asked.

"Sure, Dad." Tess looked at her father. Jim Thomas's head was well above the Jeep roof, the dimple in his chin deepening as he smiled at his daughter. He shook the tree hard to free any loose needles, then twirled it around on its trunk for Tess's inspection.

"What do you think?" he said.

The tree spun like a ballerina, perfectly poised and neatly balanced with even green needles and no brown holes. "Good job!" Tess commented.

"Tyler picked it out."

"Way to go, Ty." Tyler waved her off, but she saw a gleam of pride in his eyes as he walked into the house. They set it up on the red metal stand in the family room, spreading a gauzy white tree skirt around its base like a tutu.

"Let's get out the decorations," her mom said, carrying a wooden tray of steaming mugs into the room. Tess closed her eyes and breathed deeply. The cinnamon spice of the cider competed with the piney sap of the tree for her attention. She had forgotten the scents of Christmas.

"I'll do the lights, then you guys can each put on your own ornaments," Dad offered.

"Okay." Tess eagerly searched among the cartons and crates for her ornament box. Each year her parents bought a special ornament for her and one for Tyler, representing what had been important to them that past year. As soon as all the ornaments from the previous year were up, her mom and dad presented them with this year's.

"Look, here's my Elmo!" Tyler said. Tyler was wild for Elmo when he was five.

"And my hiking boots from last year. I still can't believe you found a hiking boot ornament," Tess giggled, hanging it on a sturdy branch.

"If you make the Rim-to-Rim this year, I'll paint a smiley face on them myself!" her dad said. Tess and her father were planning to hike from the south rim to the north rim of the Grand Canyon next May. Usually they trained for it by hiking together one evening or morning per week.

Soon the tree trimmings were hung. Tess's new ornament was a horse, since she had grown to love riding, and Tyler's was a horned toad, like Hercules, his pet.

Finally Tess opened the carton with the nativity scene. "I'll put this on the fireplace mantel," she said. One by one she lifted out the sheep, the shepherd with his curled staff, and some dried moss. Mary gazed adoringly at the manger while Joseph stood silent guard. Tess clicked on the battery-operated star that hung on the roof's eaves and dug through the wrapping for the last, most important figure.

"Where's baby Jesus?" she asked.

"I don't know. Isn't he in there?" her mother answered.

"No." Tess turned the box upside down, and all the yellowed wrapping tissue floated to the ground. But no figure was there. "We can't have Christmas without baby Jesus."

"I'm sure he'll turn up somewhere," her father said. "Why don't you carry your small tree box to your room?

I'd like to vacuum up these needles before they are dragged all over the house."

"I'll help you look after I unwrap my little tree," Tyler offered.

Tyler and Tess each had a mini-Christmas tree with mini-ornaments and tiny strings of lights that they set up in their rooms.

"Thanks, Ty. I'll meet you in my room," Tess said. She blew the dust off the empty manger and grabbed her box, taking it to her room.

A few minutes later, with her box still unopened, Tess logged into her computerized diary. The cool blue glow of the screen spread through her dark room. She wiped the dusty screen while waiting for the program to pop up.

Dear God, she started, happily writing to the Lord. A couple of months ago she just wrote, *Dear Diary*, but it seemed better to write to Someone alive than to a diary that wasn't.

> *We put up the tree tonight. It looks really nice. Did you see it? All the ornaments look good, and the lights twinkle like red, blue, and yellow stars tucked into a forest-green sky. But when I went to put up the nativity scene, baby Jesus was missing. Nobody thinks it's a big deal. Tyler knows it means a lot to me, so he's coming to help me find him. Thank you that you love us. Please help my mom and dad and brother see you like I do. And help me to sell all my cookies.*
>
> *Love, Tess*

six

Preparation

Friday Night, December 20

Erin clapped her floury hands together, and a cloud of dust fell over her and Tess. "Look! It's snowing," she said.

"Don't you look lovely." Tess giggled.

"Hey, girls, I'm getting enough gray in my hair without adding any white!" Erin's mother, Mrs. Janssen, smiled at them as she rolled out yet another batch of Christmas angels.

"Would you like some coffee?" Molly Thomas asked her, pouring herself a cup.

"Yes, thank you."

"Me, too," Tess said.

"All right, it's decaf." Tess's mom patted her slightly rounded tummy. "Baby doesn't like caffeine."

They sipped their drinks until the timer on the oven rang, announcing the shift change—one batch of cookies off the cooling racks and into their cellophane bags; one batch out of the oven to cool; and a third into the oven to bake.

"My feet hurt," Tess said. "How many are left?"

"Two more batches to the oven; then I think we're done," her mother answered. "Did you tie ribbons around the bags?"

"Yes, I put a red ribbon around the bags of four and a green ribbon around the bags of two," Tess answered.

"And I curled the ribbons with the scissors," Erin said. She zipped the scissors' edge along another ribbon, and it spiraled into ringlets.

"Where's my sample?" Tess's dad walked into the kitchen and pretended to pull some cookies off the cooling rack.

"Oh no you don't." Tess pushed him good-naturedly. "Those are fifty cents each, sir."

"Fifty cents! For poor old dad? Maybe I'll take it out of the money for your Christmas gift," he teased.

"Now, Jim," Mrs. Thomas said, smiling. "You know her gift is already purchased and hiding."

"Yeah, but if you're really nice to me, I'll give you a cookie when we're done," Tess said.

"Thank you, oh gracious one," he replied. "I think I deserve at least one since Tyler and I finished putting up the outside lights today."

Erin's mom set the next batch of cookies to cool on the rack, scooting the already cooled ones onto the counter. "Why don't we finish up the cookies while you girls make the sign for your booth? Erin and I set up my angel collection at the booth on the way over, but you still need to glue the paper angels to the hanging sign."

"Okay," Tess answered. She and Erin took the sign and the angels into the family room where Tyler sat watching TV.

After gluing the letters on the sign, Erin whispered to Tess, "Watch this." She spread a thin layer of glue over her palm and gently blew on it until it was dry. Then she peeled back a layer of the now invisible glue. A soft layer of skinlike glue peeled off.

"Cool! Let me try." Tess spread the glue over her pointer finger, up to the green painted nail.

"The polish looks great. Your parents said okay?" Erin said.

"Well, they said okay till Christmas. I wanted to buy some blue, too, but they said no way." Tess blew on her finger until the glue was dry and walked over to Tyler. "Hey, look!" She peeled back a layer of the "skin" and said, "Ouch, ouch."

"Boffo, ol' girl. How did you do that?" Tyler said. "Now you and Hercules have something in common. You both shed your skin!"

"Aren't you sicked out?" Tess said, a little disappointed.

"Sicked out? I think it's right jolly!" he answered. "Let me have some of that." He grabbed the glue.

"Do you think your folks are giving you the deposit for the Lazy K?" Erin asked.

"I'm pretty sure. I told them a long time ago, and I did

get a horse for my ornament this year. Isn't it great? This will be the best summer ever!"

"Are you kidding?" Tyler asked. "There are better things to do with a summer than spend it with a bunch of horse-crazy girls. Like watch the grass grow."

"You're just jealous," Tess said. "Tell Erin what you asked for."

"Gecko Grass and Hot Rocks," Tyler answered.

"What?" Erin asked.

"Gecko Grass makes Hercules' cage more comfy, and the Hot Rocks warm up with electricity so that they are just like the blistering stones he would find in the desert. Isn't that cool?"

"It is," Erin admitted. "My brother Josh would think that was cool, too." Josh and Tyler were in the same grade at Coronado Elementary but in different classes.

"Tess, we've just pulled the last batch out for you!" her mom called from the kitchen.

"Oh, good," Tyler said. "Now we can start making my Cricket Lickets!"

Erin looked at Tess for an explanation, but Tess shrugged her shoulders as if to say, "Who knows?" They ran into the kitchen to see the completed bags.

"Seventeen dozen." Erin's mother sat down heavily in the chair. "I'm worn out."

"Yeah, but they look great." Erin stood behind her mother and put her arm around her. "I just know they'll sell."

"I hope so," Mrs. Thomas said. Warm lemon smells filled the kitchen, and more than two hundred Christmas angels shone from their decorative bags. The overhead kitchen light glistened off the cellophane and reflected through the melted candy panels. Tess toyed with one of the bags, and it crinkled under her touch. "Tess, could you please go out to the garage and bring in some of the boxes that held the ornaments? I'll line them with waxed paper, and then we'll pack the cookies in them so they'll be easy to carry into the fair tomorrow."

"Sure. I'll be right back." Tess leaped from her chair and walked toward the garage. The garage door was still open from when Dad and Tyler had hung the lights. Two crickets chirped merrily back and forth to one another in the starlight. By the dim garage light, she rummaged around looking for empty boxes.

"No, that's not big enough," she muttered. She found two boxes but wanted to locate a third. That way they could pack the cookies lightly and not risk squashing or breaking any of them.

Moving aside one broken-down box, she noticed an old blanket lying across the top of what looked like an intact box. Tess recognized the blanket. It was old Navajo style and usually stayed in their car trunk for emergencies. Last month Tess had hidden the kitten she had bought for Erin, whom Erin had named Starlight, in that very blanket.

"Maybe there's a box under here," she said to herself, lifting it up. "Oh boy, what is this?" she said under her breath. There was a beautiful dollhouse, with perfectly carved furniture, little rugs, and a family. Quickly she looked to see if anyone had noticed her. No one seemed to be around. She sat down on a ladder rung.

A dollhouse. A really beautiful dollhouse. But not a deposit for camp. And camp with Erin was what she wanted more than anything in the whole world. Plus, well, didn't they think she was just a little too old for a dollhouse? *I mean, first they wanted Tyler to tag along with me, and now this.* She sighed. *They really do think I am a little kid.* But they had put a lot of thought into this gift, so she wouldn't spoil their surprise.

All right then, now it was even more important that all her cookies sell. With the money she would make, plus what she had saved from baby-sitting and allowance, she would have just enough to buy everyone a small present plus the deposit for summer camp at the ranch. She must get to the camp with her Secret Sister.

seven

Flirty Girty

Saturday Morning, December 21

"I'm going to stroll over to see what the Coronado Club's booth looks like," Tess said. "Can you hold the fort for a while?"

"Yeah," Erin sighed. "Hardly anybody is coming over here. And Katie and Joann will be here in a minute. Where did Tyler go?"

"One of his friends is here with his mother, and his friend is selling homemade Play-Doh. Actually, it's sort of cool. They made it with Kool-Aid so it smells really good. I might buy some for the two little boys I sometimes baby-sit."

"We should have known it was going to be really bad when they stuck us in the back. Nobody even took that booth next to us." Erin adjusted one of the raffia angels flying above their booth, courtesy of her dad's fishing line. White and yellow lights blinked a warm welcome from around their half of the booth, the "Christmas Angel" section, but there was no one to welcome.

"I know. My dad might have more cookies to eat than he thinks," Tess said glumly. "I'll be back in a few minutes." She strolled through the crowds, looking left and right at the bounty spilling over into the aisles from other booths. Holiday dolls dressed in poinsettia-red frocks, dried flower arrangements, and tea-colored rag rugs woven together in country style were displayed. Large silk cacti were swathed in red ribbon and dangled little saguaro earrings from each prickly stem. In one corner a large Santa ho-ho-hoed in loud tones, scaring away everyone under the age of six. Everyone over six was too embarrassed to sit next to him. Tess felt sorry for him, sweating in that hot suit.

One group sold hand-painted ornaments and another tiny woven stockings. Tess stopped for a minute and felt one, rubbing the soft velvet against her palm. Six inches long and edged in lace, it was perfect for a baby brother—or sister—not yet born. She noted the cost, three dollars, and decided to check back later in the day.

She tried to act casual, strolling up to booth number one, as if she were browsing and not looking at them in particular. They did have some cool stuff like personalized earrings. Since Colleen's mother was a jewelry distributor, she probably got them cheap. At least the Coronado Club wasn't selling placemats. That would have been too much.

"Ooh, look over there, Colleen. Isn't that your old

friend? You know, Tess?" Lauren waved toward Tess, who was trying to remain hidden. It hadn't worked.

"Hi, Tess, how are you?" Colleen asked. Funny, her voice sounded nice. Maybe she had caught a virus.

"I'm fine, thanks. How are sales?"

"Dreamy," Melody said. "This is the best booth ever." *Yeah, well, rub it in.*

"Not much going on toward the back, I see?" Lauren nodded toward Tess's booth. "I noticed you brought your little brother. How sweet. Did you bring your pillow and teddy bear, too?" A crowd of boys standing around the Coronado Club's booth cracked up. Embarrassed heat flooded throughout Tess's body.

"I'd better get going," she said to Colleen, ignoring Lauren and Melody. She turned on her heels and walked toward her booth. Although Colleen was never as important to her as Erin, her Secret Sister, was, it still made her sad Colleen had turned out to be such a two-face. A few moments later Tess was back at her booth as Katie and Joann set up their wares.

"Hi, Tess. Do you like our pots?" Katie and Joann placed some pretty painted pots on upside-down wooden crates. Inside some of them Christmas cacti erupted with taffy-colored blossoms among the many flat, spiny leaves.

"They look great. I'm sure they'll sell."

"How was the Coronado Club?" Erin asked.

"Those Flirty Girtys," Tess said. "Lauren has enough makeup on to support the drama club. And she was batting her eyelashes so fast at the boys that air currents were swirling around. But mostly they were selling stuff." Tess noted the lack of customers in front of her own booth.

"Hey, I almost forgot. I couldn't tell you about the doll-house last night," Tess said.

"What dollhouse?" Erin asked.

"Well, when I was out in the garage looking for boxes, I lifted up a blanket and underneath was a brand new dollhouse."

"Oh, no. For you?" Erin asked.

"Well, it's not for Tyler! It's more important than ever that we sell these cookies. Otherwise I'll have no way to pay the deposit for the Lazy K. Look who's coming." Tess jostled Erin.

It was Scott Shearin, from their class. A brown-and-gold rugby shirt set off his hazel eyes, and he had on corduroy pants instead of his usual holey jeans. "Hi, girls!" he said, polite for a change.

"Hi, Scott," Erin answered, smiling broadly and turning a delicate pink. She didn't say much else, though. Tess knew Erin liked Scott, so she assumed Erin wouldn't want him to leave the booth. But right now she seemed tongue-tied. Tess decided to step in with some conversation before it got uncomfortable.

"Want a cookie, Scott?"

"I don't have any money," he said.

"You can have one free," Tess answered. "It looks as if we'll have some extra."

"Thanks," he said, biting off a piece. "These are really good."

"They are my grandmother's recipe. Come back later, and we'll give you some more."

"Okay, I'll see you guys later." Scott walked off to catch up with another friend.

Tyler sat in the back of the booth, squishing blueberry and lime Play-Doh together to form a planet Earth. Joann and Katie were busy selling stationery—and even a pot. Turning around, Tess looked for Erin.

"Hey, what are you doing?" she asked.

"Nothing."

"What's the matter? Your face looks all red. Aren't you glad Scott came by?"

"Why should I be glad? I didn't even get a chance to talk with him."

"What do you mean?" Tess asked.

"Sure, Tess, you wouldn't let me squeeze a word in edgewise. Maybe you caught the Flirty-Girty disease over at booth one." Erin turned her back to Tess and fidgeted with the cookie bags.

I wasn't flirting! I was doing it for her, Tess thought. *But if she wants to be stuck up about it, fine. We won't talk.*

eight

Mocha Mike

Saturday Afternoon, December 21

Tess didn't have time to think through why Erin was so upset. A minute later a bear-sized man struggled down the row toward their booth, his grizzly beard wagging as he talked. "Can someone help me with this, please?"

Tess ran out into the aisle in time to catch a large box of sugar cubes about to topple off his silver cart. "Caught it!" she said triumphantly.

"Do appreciate it, miss. Name's Mocha Mike. I'm a bit late, but I'll be setting up my coffee cart in booth thirty-five, right next to you young ladies it seems." His jolly eyes sparked as he talked.

Tess stood back while he wheeled his portable espresso machine into his booth. Slipping back into her own booth, she sat down in a chair and watched Mike set up his wares. Clinking around, he settled a silver thermos labeled "Half and half" next to one labeled "Skim milk."

"From fat cows and skinny cows," he joked. Tall towers of small, medium, and large cups leaned over the left side of the cart, like cardboard Towers of Pisa. Tiny plastic spoons fanned out from a glass mug. They were stirring sticks, Tess supposed.

"You have a lot of stuff there," Tyler said. Tess stared hard at him to encourage him to be quiet. But Tyler didn't stop talking. He did something worse. He started in with the British accent.

"Say there, ol' boy, seems a fine fellow like you could use help. I'm right handy with tools." Tyler leaned over into Mocha Mike's booth.

"Come on over, young fellow," Mike answered. "You can set the bean packages in the display while I heat up the steamer." Tess wasn't too happy about Tyler's going into a stranger's booth, but she would stay right there, so she guessed it was okay.

Soon Mike had his booth in order, glistening bottles of flavored syrups standing at attention shoulder to shoulder along the top of his cart. They jostled slightly, and the cart wiggled when the steamer fired up. Big, burlap-covered barrels invited even noncoffee drinkers to inhale deeply from the endless piles of gleaming oily beans. Tess grabbed one, rubbing it between her thumb and middle finger. Some of the chocolate-colored residue stuck to her hand even after she released it.

"So you're the man in charge of these young ladies, huh?" Mocha Mike asked Tyler.

"No way. I'd rather eat grubs than sit with these guys

all day," Tyler said. "I'm only here until my mom and dad come back from the bank."

"And he's definitely not in charge of us," Joann said. She turned back as a customer came to purchase a pot.

But no one was buying the cookies. Erin still wouldn't look at Tess, but Erin did offer Mike a cookie. "Would you like to try one of our angel cookies?"

"Sure I would. They're prettier than a rabbit fur coat." Tess didn't think a rabbit fur coat sounded too pretty, but she didn't say anything.

Mike bit into the cookie and raised his eyebrows before polishing off the entire cookie. "Delicious, ladies. I do thank you. But now I'd best get back to coffee, a line is forming in front of my humble cart."

He was right. The delicate aroma of fine roasted coffee wafted across the entire fair, doing the impossible for the tiny, out-of-the-way booth.

After a minute Mike poked his head into their booth again. "Sometimes a simple fellow like me gets a barn-burner of an idea. Why don't you ladies break a few of those cookies into pieces and put them on this pretty plate? I'll offer samples to the coffee customers. Once they taste that delicate mouthful, they're sure to want more."

Erin nodded her agreement, and they opened one of the bags of four, breaking each cookie into about eight pieces. She set the plate on the front of Mocha Mike's cart, and true to his prediction, the customers started to rave.

"Where can I buy some of these cookies?" Tess heard

one customer ask. Encouragingly, the same woman came and purchased a bag after Mocha Mike pointed to the booth to his right. Before the girls knew it, they had customers lining up from Mike's booth to theirs. People bought the coffee, sampled a cookie, and came to purchase more.

"Isn't this great?" Tess elbowed Erin and giggled. *Lazy K, here I come.*

"Yes," Erin answered, but she didn't smile much.

Half an hour later Mr. Thomas came to pick up Tyler. "How's business, pal?" he asked Tess as Tyler gathered his Play-Doh.

"Great, Dad! We weren't selling anything for a while, but as soon as the coffee cart came, the smell of the coffee drew everyone back here. And now, look, half our cookies are gone!"

"Just don't forget to save one or two for the old man," he said. "We'll be back right at four to take you home."

"Okay, Dad."

One after another the customers came over. It was good for Joann and Katie, too. Since so many people came to buy cookies, many of them looked at the pots and stationery, too. With only two Christmas cacti left, Joann was busily painting names on the empty pots. She personalized each pot for the purchaser. Almost half of their handmade thank-you notes were sold.

Katie whispered to Tess, "We thought this booth was going to be so bad. I think we're getting more people than if we had been at the entrance since they're hanging around looking at our stuff while they wait for their coffee." Tess quickly agreed, then went back to selling cookies. Glancing over at Mike, she caught his broad wink and smiled back. It was so cool the way this was working out. She never would have dreamed what kind of miracles God would work when she had offered her simple prayer to sell her cookies.

"Hey, Erin . . . ," she started, wanting to share the joy with her sis. But her voice drifted off to nothing as she remembered their fight. Erin didn't turn around. Tess felt her stomach drop to the bottom of a well. The money wouldn't mean anything if she lost Erin.

nine

Parlez-vous Français?

Saturday Afternoon, December 21

"If you don't mind, I think I'll walk around again. I want to see if that stocking I found for the baby is still for sale," Tess said.

Erin nodded but didn't answer.

Why was she so mad? Couldn't she understand that Tess didn't care about talking to Scott except to keep him at the booth for Erin? Obviously not. Blood rushed to Tess's face and stayed there, as if she wore a too-tight turtleneck. And her nose felt tingly. This was so upsetting, their first fight. It would be a total waste if their great friendship—and sisterhood—was ruined over a stupid boy. Tess waved to Mocha Mike as she left the booth, and he waved back. She had a gift to buy.

"I wonder if it'll be a boy or a girl," she said aloud, trying to decide between the stockings that were edged in lace and those edged in plaid. Ever since her parents had told her about the baby, Tess had been thinking about it. Would she have to baby-sit all the time? Mom wasn't going to quit working, and even though she worked at home, Tess helped out with Tyler. What if everybody became so busy with the baby they didn't have time for her? And it was sort of embarrassing that her mom was having another baby. She might be getting a little too old for that kind of thing. But it would be fun for Tess to have her own little snuggle bunny. And she could teach the baby all kinds of things.

"I'll take this one." She handed a delicate velvet stocking the color of maraschino cherries to the lady at the booth. It was edged in snowy cotton velour, perfect for either a girl or a boy. Baby wouldn't use it this year, of course, but he or she was here, after all. After tucking away the small brown bag with her purchase inside her backpack, she couldn't help but sneak over toward the Coronado Club booth again. This time she hid herself better.

No way! Could that be Tom talking to Lauren? Tess knew that Tom, Erin's brother, was coming with her mom toward the end of the fair to take Erin home, but she didn't know that he knew Lauren. More determined than ever to hear what was being said, she moved closer.

From just behind an earring display in booth three, Tess heard Lauren speaking what sounded like a foreign language, and Colleen interpreting. Tess knew that Colleen didn't speak a foreign language. In fact, she had told Tess she hoped she never had to learn one since English was hard enough for her. Jealousy spread through Tess as she watched Tom smile at Lauren. Tess noted that their booth was still half-full of their wares. They had sold some items, but some were still left. A little confused over the language, she left booth three and walked back to her own.

Once there, she rearranged Tyler's Cricket Lickets in the upside-down cone he had poked holes into to display his insect candy. She tried not to touch the buggy things too much. They sicked her out, frozen in time as they were in a syrupy sucker. But she was sorry she would have to take them home and disappoint her brother. Moving the cone to the front of the booth, she hoped they would attract attention in the last five minutes of the show. Erin busied herself selling the last few bags of cookies.

"We're done!" Katie said. "We sold all the stationery and all but two of the pots, which Joann is keeping to give to her aunt for Christmas." Joann's paintbrush dipped and swirled through the air, gracefully spelling out her aunt's name.

"That is so great. I think we sold everything, too. I'll have to ask Erin," Tess replied.

"What's the matter with her?" Katie continued. "She's hardly said anything all afternoon."

Tess shrugged her shoulders and walked toward the front of the booth just as Tom and his friends arrived. Tom's golden hair curled slightly around his head, a tiny cowlick twirling a lock back from his forehead. Like Erin, he had dimples, and they spread as he smiled. Tess could barely answer him as he asked, "How were sales today?"

"F-fine," she said.

"I saw you a few minutes ago," he continued, "looking at earrings a few booths down from that foreign girl's booth. You looked busy so I didn't want to interrupt."

Oh no, he had seen her! But she was pretty sure Lauren hadn't, since her back had been toward Tess. "What do you mean, foreign girl?" she asked. Erin moved closer to listen.

"Hi, Sis," he said to her, then turned back to Tess. "You know, Lauren, the French girl."

"She's not French! She goes to Coronado," Tess said.

"No kidding!" Tom replied. "Her friend said she couldn't speak English and translated what she said for me."

"Sounds just like them." Erin elbowed Tess, forgetting for a minute that they were fighting. Tess smiled back at her, but Erin must have remembered, because she turned away from Tess. "I'll count the money," she said.

"I guess I'll start picking up the booth," Tess answered, grabbing the Cricket Licket cone.

"What are those?" Tom asked. His friend Brandon moved in closer to see, too.

"They're clear mint suckers with real crickets in the middle," Tess explained. "My brother thought they would sell."

"No way, real crickets?" Tom asked. "Hey, Brandon, check it out." They each picked one up and held it to the light to look closer at the insect inside.

"These are awesome," Brandon said. "The team would love them!" Tess gathered that Brandon must play on the middle school basketball team with Tom.

"How much are they?"

"A dollar fifty each," Tess answered.

"We'll take them all. Want to split the cost with me?" Tom asked his friend. Brandon nodded, and between them they handed Tess eighteen dollars.

"Tell your brother thanks. These are great." Tom beamed a megawatt smile at Tess. She could only nod back.

"Mom and I will meet you in front," Tom said to Erin, who waved an okay back at him.

Tess tried to make up. "Can you believe what they said about the Coronado Club? That Lauren was speaking French?"

"Too incredible," Erin said.

Mocha Mike leaned over but apparently had heard only part of the conversation. "A French girl in booth one, huh? My mom was French, and I haven't had a chance to converse in that language for a good number of years. I think I'll mosey over and strike up a conversation."

"Wait . . . ," Tess started to say, but she was too late. Mike hustled up to the front. She and Erin looked at one another, then followed at a safe distance.

When Mike approached booth one, Lauren and Colleen were packing up their leftover crafts. Melody fixed her hair, looking in a hand mirror. From a few feet away the girls could hear Mike start a conversation. *"Bonjour,"* he said. *"Je parle français, et je comprend qu'il ya-t-une française ici. Ou est elle?"*

Colleen backed away, but Lauren stood up, shaken. "Pardon me?" she said quietly.

"I understand there's a French girl here," Mike continued. "I'd love to speak with her. My mother was French," he continued proudly. "Are you she?" He turned toward Lauren and Colleen. *"Parlez-vous français?"* he asked.

Lauren stood mute for a minute before stammering, "There must be some mistake. I'm not French."

"Sorry, miss. There must be. Didn't mean to disturb you." Mike backed away and bowed with a flourish. Tess and Erin giggled together for a minute, careful to stay in the background. They headed back toward their booth well ahead of Mocha Mike.

"I feel a little sorry for Lauren. She looked so tongue-tied," Tess whispered. "I guess it's true that lies will find you out." Tess nudged her friend, hoping Erin had forgiven her. But Erin only smiled a little, then went back to counting the money.

Tess thought she would try one last time. "Do you want me to ask my mom and dad to drive me to church tomorrow?" She hoped Erin would say no, that she would pick up Tess as always.

"If you think that would be okay," Erin answered, looking down but handing Tess her stack of cash.

"Sure." Tess slowly took the money, her heart sinking. It didn't matter if she made enough for camp. Erin probably wouldn't want to go with her anymore. And Tess didn't want to go without her.

Ten Percent

Sunday, December 22

"Are you sure things are okay between Erin and you?" Tess's mom asked. "It seems strange that you would want me to drive you this morning. Not that I mind," she added quickly.

"I don't know. I think Erin is mad at me because I talked to this kid yesterday. It's a silly misunderstanding, but she won't make up."

"That doesn't sound like Erin," her mother said. "Why don't you try talking with her this morning?"

"Maybe," Tess said. "I tried that yesterday, and it didn't work." She felt that she had tried to make up a couple of times, and now it was up to Erin. After all, Tess hadn't really done anything wrong. But she didn't want to be in a fight anymore either.

A few minutes later Tess and her mom pulled up in front of Living Water Community Church. Tess opened the Jeep door, reminding her mother to pick her up in an hour and a half. Walking past the jumping cholla, Tess was careful not to come too close to the springing cacti. They could sense she was there and would spring their darty needles at her. Hundreds of waxy gray leaves dotted twiggy olive branches, quietly moving in the gentle wind. Olive trees, which made her dad sneeze in the springtime, lined the sidewalk leading to the church's main entrance. A cheerful greeter shook her hand as Tess came through the open door and into the church.

The spacious hallways were crowded. Tess tried to make her way to the sixth-grade Sunday school classroom. Stopping for a minute at the drinking fountain, she looked above it and saw a wooden box with a brass plate that read "Tithes and Offerings." *Hmmm.*

"Excuse me," a man said to Tess, leaning toward the fountain.

"Oh, sorry." She scooted out of the way and headed toward her classroom. Still thinking about the sign, Tess remembered getting a drink a couple of weeks ago and asking Erin's mom about the tithes and offerings box.

"A tithe is the first 10 percent of any money you earn or receive as a gift," Mrs. Janssen had explained. "The Bible says that it belongs to the Lord, as thanks that he provides everything. An offering is anything above that 10 percent. The box is one place where you can deposit your tithes and offerings."

Tess touched the hard lump of her wallet through the soft case of her Bible cover, then walked into the classroom.

"Tess, come over here," her new friend Melissa called to her. Melissa's wavy red hair, pulled back in a jaws clip, cascaded between her shoulder blades. Fair freckles sprinkled her creamy skin, and her green eyes smiled. Last month Melissa had invited Tess to work with her and her mother in the toddler nursery once a month. Tess loved kids, so it was no problem.

"Sorry to grab you just as you walked in," she whispered, keeping her voice down as the teacher started to talk. "But I wanted to know if you could do nursery duty with me on Christmas Eve."

Tess took a seat next to Melissa, scanning the room for Erin. There she was. Locking eyes with her for a minute, Tess thought she saw Erin's eyes fill with tears before they abruptly turned away.

"Um, what? Sorry, I wasn't paying attention," Tess said.

"Can you work the nursery with my mom and me on Christmas Eve?" Melissa repeated. "Usually tons of kids are there, and we could use the help."

"I'm not sure," Tess said. "I don't know if my family is coming or not. I'll check this afternoon and call you, okay?"

"Sure. Still have my phone number?"

"Yep, it's tacked up on my bulletin board."

"Okay. Hey, a minute before you walked in, Sjana asked us to break into small circles. Do you want to be in mine?"

Tess felt torn. She liked Melissa, but she wanted to

talk with Erin, and there might not be another chance until the end of class.

Sjana, one of their teachers, put an end to Tess's speculation. "Okay, now that you're in small circles, I want you guys to brainstorm some ways to keep Christ in Christmas."

Tess liked Sjana and thought it was cool that she spelled her name with a *j* instead of plain "Shauna," when she wrote it on the board. Well, it looked as if Tess was staying put.

Melissa and Tess sat with four others. One boy Tess didn't know spoke first. "Last year my family went through our toys and gave away at least one old toy for every new one we received as a present."

"That's a great idea," Robin said. "My cousins choose a name from a tree at the mall and buy that kid whatever present he asked for. Usually they're kids who don't have too much."

"I looked up the word *give* in the back of my Bible," Melissa said.

Tess nodded. That sounded good. Maybe she would do that, too.

She thought about sharing her plan to spend five dollars for a needy child through the Christmas Angel program. But she didn't want to sound as if she was bragging or anything. She had never spoken up in small circle before.

The others were just sitting there, and suddenly she felt she had to say something. Sweat covered her palms, but her voice squeaked out anyway. "When I was putting up my manger scene, I noticed that baby Jesus was missing. I thought, that's how Christmas used to be for me. I saw everything else but didn't see Jesus."

Everyone sat quietly, and Tess hung her head. *Well, now you've done it,* she thought. *Your first time to speak up, and you sound like a goody two shoes. Whatever made you say something?*

"That is so true," one girl offered. When Tess raised her head, she saw that each one in the small circle was nodding agreement. "I think you should tell that story to Sjana," the girl continued.

"Um, maybe," Tess said shyly. But with a little pride. She might not be ready to tell Sjana about the manger story, though.

"Last year I got in-line skates, which I hated," Albert said. "I wanted trading cards. But I didn't say anything, because I knew my grandma tried really hard." Heads nodded, including Tess's.

Soon small group was over, and they had worship, song, and prayer time. Sjana and Ted taught a lesson about the first Christmas. Afterward, as the group stood up, Tess reminded Melissa, "I'll call you later to let you know about Christmas Eve."

"Okay, thanks. It was fun to be in your small circle."

"Yeah, you, too," Tess agreed. She turned away, looking for Erin, but she couldn't see her in the rapidly emptying room. Erin must have left without saying good-bye.

Well, that was rude. Tess couldn't believe how Erin was acting. Being mad was one thing, but not even making up at church today was another.

Slowly lifting the blue-jeans Bible case that Erin had given her last month, Tess pulled out some Sugar Plum lip gloss. Had Erin brought her Hot Chocolate lip gloss today in her Bible case pocket? Had she missed sitting together this morning? Would they ever sit together again?

As Tess tucked the lip gloss away, she felt her wallet again. Setting her Bible down, she opened up the wallet and peeled off a five-dollar bill. Since she had made fifty dollars yesterday, it was only right to give her very first tithe. That money had seemed so hard to make. But God had helped her. She did have lots of money left over, after all. As she walked out of the church, she slipped her tithe into the box above the drinking fountain.

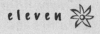

eleven

Pool of Cash

Sunday Evening, December 22

"Dad, have you thought about Christmas Eve?" Tess asked, scrubbing dried tomato sauce off the kitchen table with a hot dishcloth.

"What about it?" her dad asked, rewarming his coffee in the microwave. A few seconds later he pulled out the steaming mug and took a sip, waiting for Tess to continue.

"Well, I mean about going to church." Talking about church was always harder with her dad than with her mother. Grandpa Pat, her mother's dad, had been a Christian, and last month Tess had even found his Bible. That made it a little easier to approach her mom with spiritual things. But her dad was different.

"You mean, may you go to church? I don't see why not. Erin's family can pick you up, right?"

"I guess they could," Tess continued. Draping the dishcloth over the faucet, she pulled up a chair next to him and nibbled a chocolate-chip cookie. Dad dunked his cookie in his coffee, which Tess thought was gross. Then he had soggy cookie crumbs floating belly up in his drink. Yuck.

"Well . . . ?" her dad said, motioning her to continue.

"It's just that there isn't any Sunday school on Christmas. Everyone is in the big service. With their families," she finished, staring intently at her cookie.

"I see. And you want us to come with you."

"Yes. I don't want to be alone."

"You know how I feel about church, Tess. I think it's fine for you to attend as long as you don't get crazy and your grades stay up. But it's not for me."

"Why not?" Tess asked, speaking aloud the question she had silently considered for the past month or two.

"I've just never been religious, Tess. I don't know why. My parents went on Christmas and Easter but didn't do much else, and that seemed silly to me. I didn't see the point, and I didn't want to raise my family that way. So I stopped going."

"I would really like to go, Dad. And Melissa wants me to work in the nursery with her one hour. So you could drop me off, and then we could meet for the second service. Could you think about it?"

"I'll consider it, Tess. Now, I believe you told your brother you would meet him in his room as soon as you had cleaned the kitchen." Her father kissed the top of her head and took his coffee into the family room to catch the game on TV.

She had tried. Walking down the hall, she knocked

on Tyler's door as he had asked her to do. "Anybody home?"

"Come on in," he answered. "Just feeding the H-Monster."

"Oh, is that Hercules' new name?" Tess said, leaning over the cage. Hercules rolled his beady yellow eyes at her, and she stuck her tongue out at him. Mimicking her, he lashed his tongue in and out. "Gross," Tess said, pulling away.

"Just one more cricket, and the ol' fella will have dined sufficiently." Tyler shook the final fat cricket into the cage. The cricket tried to escape, but it was the death penalty. The horned toad swallowed him alive in one huge gulp.

"So what did you want to talk about?" Tess asked.

Fixing the lid on Hercules' cage, Tyler motioned her over to his bed. "I was afraid I wasn't going to have any money to buy Christmas gifts, but since you did such a great job selling my Cricket Lickets, I guess we have a pool of cash. What should we buy Mom and Dad?"

"I don't know," Tess said. "I was thinking maybe a restaurant gift certificate or something."

"Yeah, but how are we going to get to the restaurant to buy one of those?" Tyler asked.

"That's true," Tess agreed. "We'll probably have to buy something at Smitty's while they're in another department. How about a pregnancy exercise video?"

"Oh, yeah, great for Dad," Tyler said. "I don't think so. How about an automatic golf scorer?"

"Oh, yeah, great for Mom," Tess laughed. "I don't

know. Hey, here's an idea. Dad is taking us to the mall tomorrow to shop. I could leave you two for a minute and find something really cool there."

"You mean leave the three of us?" Tyler asked.

"No, Mom isn't coming. Just you, Dad, and me."

"And Big Al."

"Uh-uh. No way," Tess said.

"Actually, Mom said he could come since I had to sit at the girl craft fair on Saturday. So, ol' pal, looks like you're pickled."

"Even more reason to leave you guys alone! Does that idea sound okay?"

"Yeah, I trust you to find something good. But no lady stuff, okay?"

"Okay," Tess agreed. She stood up and gave Tyler a high-five before heading into her own room.

But before she could open her door, her dad called, "Tess, come here for a minute."

Tess went to the family room. "Yeah, Dad?"

"We talked about it and decided it would be okay to go to church with you on Christmas Eve. It isn't going to turn into a regular thing, but I don't mind this once."

"Okay! Thanks, Dad." Tess smiled, leaned over, and kissed his cheek, catching a whiff of his spicy after-shave.

"You're welcome."

"I'm going to my room now, okay?"

Mom nodded her approval, and her father seemed not to notice. He was more interested in the score on TV.

Once in her room, Tess logged into her diary-prayer journal.

Dear God,

Great news. My parents said they would come to church with me on Christmas Eve. I really hope they like it. I hope I like it, too. I've only gone to the big service once. But I want to focus on you at Christmas. It's your birthday, after all!

She stopped for a minute, remembering last year when she had shared her birthday party with cousin Jane. Jane's birthday was only two weeks after Tess's, and all the relatives were together already. It had seemed as if nobody paid Tess any attention. They didn't even write her name on the cake. It just had waxy pink roses.

Anyway, I think I know how you feel when we forget about you on your birthday and concentrate on our stuff instead. Now for the bad news. Erin and I didn't make up. I sure hope our friendship isn't over. It makes me feel like crying. My heart actually hurts. I wanted to call her and tell her about everyone coming to church with me, but I can't. I want to be sisters forever. I just don't know what to do next. Please tell me. And help me be nice to (yuck) Big Al tomorrow.

Love, Tess

twelve

Christmas Found

Monday, December 23

Tess sat at the breakfast table while strong winter sunlight streamed in golden rays over the newspaper. She didn't always read the comics, but on a lazy Christmas vacation day she had time. Shoveling cornflakes in one spoonful after the next, she hardly heard her mother come into the room.

"Good morning, Miss Sunshine. How are you today?" Her mother ran some water into the squat teakettle and set it on the stove.

"Fine, Mom. Getting ready to write my last Christmas cards. I guess they'll be late again. Then I'm going to make my wrapping paper." Tess smiled. This year she was creating her own gift wrap, drawing pictures on plain white paper. Instead of tags she would write on the wrapping paper. "What are you going to do while we're at the mall?"

"Odds and ends. Finish writing an ad piece so I can

e-mail the copy before Christmas. Wrap a few last-minute gifts. Take a nap." Her mother stretched and smiled.

"Did you do any laundry yesterday?" Tess asked. "I sort of wanted to wear my jeans and the white Arizona State sweatshirt today."

"Folded on top of the dryer. Could you put everyone's laundry away before you go, please?" Her mom poured some cornflakes into a bowl for herself. "Have you and Erin made up yet?"

"No. Why?" Tess turned the newspaper page.

"I care about you and your pal, honey. But also I had an idea for those placemats you guys weren't able to sell." Mrs. Thomas poured milk over her cereal.

"What's your idea?" Tess asked, penciling the easy words in the newspaper crossword puzzle. She never could get more than a few right answers.

"Well, when I was at Smitty's yesterday, I donated a meal, just like you did the other day. Then, when I was reading the newspaper later in the day, I saw that the mission that receives those free meals was offering Christmas dinner to the homeless people downtown. I thought maybe you and I could go there tomorrow and take those placemats. I'll bet they don't have a lot of decorations since they spent their money on the food."

"Do you think they would even want the placemats? I mean, a bunch of old men?"

"Homeless people aren't all old men, Tess. And even old men like beautiful things."

"Oh. Okay. I'll call Erin later and ask her if that's okay. I'd be glad not to throw them away." She wondered if Erin would even talk to her. And that meant going over to Erin's house to pick up the placemats.

"I'll call the mission to see if they want them." Mrs. Thomas got up and poured some boiling water into her mug from the now-screeching kettle. She dipped a mint tea bag into the water and left it to steep. "Is that the mail carrier already? So early. Must have extra people working for Christmas. Since I'm still in my robe, could you please get the mail for me? Maybe we received some more Christmas cards."

"Sure." Tess folded up the paper and walked to the end of the driveway. She pulled a handful of cards out of the mailbox. A miracle! One had her name on it. Maybe it was from Erin. Nope, Tess recognized the stationery as some of Joann and Katie's; so it must be from one of them. Sighing, she rifled through the rest of the mail. Another miracle! A second letter with her name on it. This one was from the Christmas Angel program. She walked back into the kitchen.

"Here's yours, Mom." She handed a big stack to her mother.

"Good, we need a few more clipped up on our line." Each year her mother strung a red clothesline across the back wall in the living room and clipped the Christmas cards to the line with green clips. That way, they could read them several times without losing them. Also they looked pretty, like tiny cardboard towels flapping on the line in the wind.

"I got two cards. One from Katie." Tess smiled, reading the inside. She would have to remember to send one to Katie, too.

"Who's the other one from?"

"That Christmas Angel program I told you about last week. Remember?"

"My goodness, that was fast. Open it up."

Tess ripped the back of the envelope and pulled out the paper.

"I'll read it aloud," Tess said. "Dear Miss Thomas, thank you very much for generously agreeing to contribute fifty dollars toward the Christmas Angel program." She stopped reading and shrieked, "Fifty dollars!" Tess sank into her chair.

Her mother's eyes grew wide, but she nodded at Tess to keep reading. "Not only will your funds go toward giving a gift to a needy child, but we're planning to build a water-purifying plant for several Central American villages so they'll have fresh water all year long. Please return this sheet of paper with your remittance. Reaching out with you in Jesus' name, The Christmas Angels."

"Tess, you didn't tell them you would send fifty dollars, did you?"

"No, no, I wrote five dollars. There's been a mistake. They must have read it wrong. What am I going to do? I have lots of plans for the money I've earned!"

"Well, don't worry. We can give them a call, or even just enclose a note with your five dollars, telling them there was an error. In fact, if you want me to, I'll write a check for five dollars. That's much safer than sending cash. And you can give me your five-dollar bill."

"Oh, I don't know. I just don't know. I guess I'll go to my room for a while. I have to think about this. And I haven't set up my small tree yet because I've been so busy with the craft fair."

"Don't forget the laundry," her mother reminded her. Like a forklift, Tess slid her arms beneath the laundry pile and then unloaded a few items in each room. Finally reaching her own, she flopped down on her bed.

What should she do? "Lord, what do you want me to do? I only meant to give them five dollars, but they think I'm sending fifty. Do you think they already made plans for it? Or sent it already? If I send them the fifty dollars, I'll have enough to buy something for Mom and Dad, Tyler and Erin—if she still wants a present. But I won't have anything left over for the Lazy K."

She didn't hear anything back. Thinking about what Melissa had said in Sunday school, Tess looked up *give* in the back of her Bible. Cool, maps were back there, too. She read a few of the verses and then came to 1 Timothy 6:17-18. She read: "Give this command to those who are rich with things of this world. Tell them not to be proud. Tell them to hope in God, not their money. Money cannot be trusted, but God takes care of us richly. He gives us everything to enjoy. Tell the rich people to do good and to be rich in doing good deeds. Tell them to be happy to give and ready to share."

But who were the rich people? Not her family. They

lived in a medium-sized house in a middle-sized neighborhood. Tess thought about the little girl on the Christmas Angels brochure. That girl didn't even have clean water. "I guess, compared to her, I'm rich," she murmured to herself. *But am I happy to give and ready to share?* Troubled by the thought, she jotted down part of the verse on a scrap of her Christmas wrap and tacked it to her bulletin board. "God takes care of us richly. He gives us everything to enjoy."

It was too quiet. She put on her CD of the new rock mix of "Little Drummer Boy" and opened the small box with her minitree. She lifted out the tree, the small string of lights, and the tiny ornaments. An eggroll-shaped package lay in the bottom of the box. Unwrapping the yellowed newspaper, she smiled with delight at what she found. Baby Jesus.

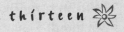

thirteen

Madcap Mall

Monday, December 23

"Look at all these people!" Tess's dad whistled as he, Tess, Tyler, and Big Al made their way through the crowded mall. "What on earth was I thinking coming here today?"

"Really. Do you think there's anything left to buy?" Tyler asked.

"There's always something to buy," his dad answered. "They stock up before Christmas, trust me."

"Incoming, incoming," Big Al called in his best air-traffic-controller voice.

"Incoming what?" Tess asked, remembering that she was going to be nice to Big Al and controlling her irritation.

"Ladies and gentlemen, fasten your seat belts and prepare for a rough landing. P.U. airlines has just encountered some turbulence." And with that, Big Al opened wide. Out of the yawning gulch of his mouth came a loud belch.

Tyler giggled. "Hi ho, old boy, splendid. Saving that one up, were you?"

"You know it," Al said.

Tess rolled her eyes, then turned her head as she heard someone call her name. Joann was waving at Tess as Joann dragged her dad in Tess's direction.

"Must be men's shopping day." Tess's dad smiled at Mr. Waters.

"I'm so glad to see another girl!" Joann said. "Nothing against you, Daddy." Tess noticed Joann squeezing her father's hand and her dad smiling before squeezing it back and letting go.

"Do you want to shop with us for a while?" Joann asked. "I'm almost done, and we're not meeting Katie and her dad for another hour. I'd really like your opinion on what to buy her."

"I'd love it! Dad, can I please meet you guys in an hour?" Tess pleaded. She had to get away from Big Al. Plus, she needed to buy her gifts, and she didn't want Dad and Tyler around for that.

"Is it okay with you?" Mr. Thomas asked Joann's father.

"Sure, no problem," Mr. Waters answered. "We'll meet you in the food court in an hour."

Tess agreed and set out to buy her gifts. What was she going to buy? She had a lot of money, ninety dollars, including the money she had saved from baby-sitting and the craft fair. Plus, Tyler had given her ten more dollars so they could spend twenty dollars on Mom and Dad. She planned on ten dollars each for Tyler and Erin. But she wanted to spend some of the money fast. Carrying so much made her nervous.

"Can we go to the pet store first?" Tess asked Joann.

"Sure," Joann said. A few minutes later they dawdled in front of the pet shop windows. The puppies were barking excitedly at the kids tapping the window. One of the dogs tried to lick the girls' palms through the glass.

"Hi, fella." Tess studied a yellow lab puppy, wishing she could have a pet. She supposed she could have another fish, but Goldy's bowl wasn't really big enough for two. And her mother had reminded her last month that they would have their hands full soon enough, with a new baby.

So it was okay just to play with Starlight, Erin's kitten. Last month, when Erin's horse died, Tess had bought Starlight to help Erin get over the pain. Thinking about Erin and their broken friendship pained Tess. Her heart beat fast again and seemed to crack inside her chest. Maybe she could find a card at the mall, one that would explain that she hadn't meant to do anything bad and that would tell Erin how much Tess missed her. Before their fight, they had talked on the phone every night. The past two nights had seemed really lonely without that.

"Yoo-hoo! Are you there?" Joann waved her hand in front of Tess.

"Sorry, just daydreaming," Tess answered.

"Are you done here? Where else do you want to go?"

"I need to buy a couple of things for my brother here. Then I guess we can go to the card shop," Tess answered. "How about you?"

"I want to go to the department store to find a shirt for Katie. And you could find something for Erin there, too."

Tess didn't say anything. She didn't want Joann to know she was fighting with Erin.

They wandered around the card shop for a while, Tess looking for something cute, but she didn't see anything. "Let's go," she finally said, and Joann agreed.

Once inside the department store, Tess saw a crowd gathered around a display. Curious, she wandered over. A salesclerk sat on a chair, pants legs rolled up to the knees, with his bare feet in some kind of machine. Tess read the box, "Sole Soother." *Hmm.*

"Ladies and gentlemen, I absolutely give you my promise, and Dan Daniels never lies, that everyone on your list will love the Sole Soother. Plug it in, pour in some warm water and our special tea, and turn it on. Your loved one will settle his or her feet into a luxury formerly known only at expensive spas. Tiny plastic fingers vibrate from below, massaging the foot and soothing the sole. Our patent-pending warmer promises to keep the water warm for as long as your feet are willing."

This might not be a bad idea. Mom's feet were always tired at the end of the day, and it would be great for Dad after hiking. Tess picked up the box—$19.95. A bargain. She walked around, looking for a salesclerk with fewer than a hundred people in line. Maybe she would go to the jewelry department. The lines weren't so long there.

"I'm going to pay over here," she called to Joann. Joann and her dad stepped just across the aisle to the junior department where Joann chose a shirt for Katie.

As Tess approached the counter, a charm display caught her eye. Tess and Erin wore matching charm bracelets that had exactly the same charms. That way, when they sealed a deal, they switched bracelets. The bracelets belonged to both of them, like twins. Tess saw a lone angel charm swinging from the display. The angel reminded her of Erin and their Christmas cookie craft booth. But there weren't two. It would be the first time one of them had a charm that the other one didn't.

Did she have enough money? Well, yes. If she bought this and nothing else, she would have $60 left over—$50 for the ranch and $10 to spend for herself.

"May I help you, miss?" A long-nosed saleslady pointed toward the Sole Soother.

"Um, yes. Do you have any more of these?" Tess pointed at the lone charm.

"I'm sorry, we don't. Would you like that one?"

Tess checked her watch. Maybe buying separate charms was a sign that she and Erin were about to go separate ways. But it was almost time to meet Dad and the boys; she might not have another chance to buy Erin a present. "Yes, I'll take it. And this." She lifted the foot massager onto the counter. Soon she, Joann, and Mr. Waters were back at the food court meeting the guys.

❄

After they arrived home, Mom told Tess, "The mission would love the placemats. But we'll need to take them tomorrow. Did you ask Erin if it was okay?"

"Um, no, but I will," Tess answered.

"Why not?" Her mom turned to look at Tess. "You two aren't still in a fight, are you?"

"I guess so."

"Well, why don't you be the one to mend things?" Her mom turned off the TV. "You better give her a call. We'll need to run by and pick them up in about half an hour if it's okay with them. I have too much to do tomorrow to go by there before we drop them off at the mission."

"Why should I have to make up? I'm not the one who started this," Tess said.

"Does it really matter? Even if you didn't start it, you can sure be the one to end it. That's how it worked between my sister and me," her mom said, which reminded Tess that she and Erin considered themselves sisters.

"Okay. I'll call." Tess went into the kitchen and picked up the phone, pressing Erin's number in the keypad, knowing where to put her fingers without even looking.

"Hello, Mrs. Janssen? Is Erin there?" Tess's heart was thumping wildly in her chest.

"No, Tess, she's out shopping with her grandma and grandpa. May I take a message?"

"Well, it's about the placemats," Tess answered. "My mom thought it would be a good idea to donate them to the homeless mission downtown for their Christmas dinner. We would need to come by to pick them up tonight so we can deliver them. Do you think Erin would mind?"

"Not at all. It's a wonderful idea. You may stop by to pick them up anytime. I'm sorry you'll miss Erin, though. She'll be at her grandparents' house until late."

"Well, yes. I'm sorry I miss her. I mean, I'll miss her," Tess blushed at the error. She did miss Erin. "We'll be by in about half an hour."

"Okay, see you then."

Tess heard the line click as Mrs. Janssen hung up. No sisterly reunion tonight.

fourteen

Light the Way

Tuesday Afternoon, December 24

"It's a little scary, isn't it?" Tess asked her mother as they pulled up at the mission house. A layer of blue paint peeled back from the concrete structure revealed a layer of ivory with bare wall beneath. Several unshaven men with shopping carts stood outside the entrance. A strong, pungent smell assaulted her nose as the wind blew past the men and toward the Jeep's open windows. Tess felt a little nervous, realizing they would have to walk past the men to go inside.

"It's okay," her mother answered. "The house mother is expecting us." She parked the Jeep curbside and, after checking to make sure the street was clear, got out. Tess followed her lead and met her on the sidewalk. Her mother grabbed the big cardboard box from the back of the Jeep. As they walked inside, Tess sidestepped the sleeping-bag rolls and piles of cigarette butts, but no one talked to her. Instead, they quietly parted to let her and her mother pass.

Her nose wrinkled in distaste as she walked quickly without looking to either side. Once inside, she was surprised to find that many of the people eating the simple soup lunch were women and children. Long rows of metal tables stretched side by side with hard-backed chairs tucked underneath. A few of the chairs were empty, but most of them were filled. No tablecloths adorned the tables, but several did have small potted poinsettias on them. Most of the kids looked as if their clothes were either too small or too big. They needed haircuts, too. But they sat next to their mothers and smiled. One girl offered a shy, silent wave to Tess. Tess smiled and waved back, overcome with the desire to offer this small girl something to really help her.

A tidy, grandmotherly woman with a white apron wiped her hands on a towel and came forward to meet them. "You must be the Thomases," she said. "I'm Anne, the house mother here. Chet is in the back. I told him I'd meet you."

"Here are our placemats," Tess offered timidly after her mother nudged her. "We made them for a craft fair but then couldn't sell them after all. Can you use them here?"

"By golly, we sure can!" Anne chuckled. "We have precious little in the way of cheer, but we do our best! Our donated tree is over in the corner, and Chet is sorting through some gifts for the children. But these placemats will warm up the special dinner we have planned. And we'll use them next year, too. Thank you, young lady."

"You're welcome," Tess answered. "Do you always have kids here?"

"Yes, the women and families eat first, then the single men. We have several seatings each night, usually with soup, rolls, and milk, or maybe spaghetti. But we have a real feast planned for tomorrow." She beamed. "Roast turkey, mashed potatoes, peas, cranberries, and pie for dessert."

Tess pointed at the young girl who had waved to her when she walked in and asked, "Where does that little girl live?"

"Who?" Anne asked.

Tess pointed again.

"Oh, Wendy. She and her family live in a shelter nearby. She's a smart one, that girl."

After a few minutes of small talk, Tess's mother said, "We better be going home. Dad is waiting for you to hike with him this afternoon."

Anne shook their hands again. "Thank you, and God bless you."

Passing the silent Wendy on the way out, Tess smiled and waved at her one last time. How thankful she was to have a home to go to. Remembering the part of the verse that had said, "Be rich in doing good deeds, happy to give and ready to share," she knew what she wanted to do about the Christmas Angel program.

Later that afternoon a wide periwinkle sky cast no

shadow over Tess and her father as they hiked up the steep trail of Squaw Peak.

"So this is why you wanted to come here today instead of hiking the Dreamy Draw," Tess said, lightly tapping one of the brown bags resting alongside the trail. Inside was a candle and a cupful of sand to anchor the bag from any light breezes that might blow.

"Yes, I thought that maybe on our way down the luminarias would light our way," her dad said.

Tess smiled. Each year for Christmas hundreds of luminarias necklaced the trail up the side of Squaw Peak like tiny beads of candlelight flickering against the graceful throat of the mountain.

"How was your visit downtown?" her father asked.

"Sort of scary and sort of sad. Kids were eating there. I didn't realize there are homeless kids, too."

"I know. Makes you feel glad to do what you can, doesn't it?" her father asked, wiping the sweat from the back of his neck with a small towel he carried on his hiking belt.

"Yeah." Tess stopped for a minute to catch her breath and retie her bootlace. Certain that the lace was tight and wouldn't come undone, she stood up and stretched.

When Tess was a little kid, she could never understand why it didn't snow on Christmas. If you watched TV, you saw all the snowmen, snowflakes, and cold people shivering amid blankets on the way to Grandma's. For a while, she didn't believe it was actually Christmas since where she lived it was warm and sunny.

"Do you ever miss the snow, Dad?" she asked. Her dad had grown up in Minnesota, where it snowed a lot.

"Not really. I think it would have been fun for you guys to go sledding more often than on just an occasional visit up north, and missing school on snow days was fun. Snow at Christmas is nice but not necessary."

"I think snow at Christmas would be cool, like a real Christmas," Tess answered. "It's weird having Christmas in the desert."

"You know, Tess, the first Christmas took place in a desert, in Bethlehem. No snow."

"You're right! I never thought about that." Tess felt better, thinking this might look more like what baby Jesus saw.

They reached the top, and she sat down on a smooth, iron-rich rock next to the rock her dad plopped onto. "Thanks again for going to church with me tonight," she said.

"I know it means a lot to you. It's fine with me," Dad said.

"Look over there." Tess pointed as two chubby quail scurried into the sage scrub nearby. Their fat little heads bobbed under cover, black feathers springing from their crowns like Yankee Doodle's plume. Tess always thought their faces, with wide black circles edged with thin white lines, looked like Oreos.

"Cute, aren't they?" her dad said. "Now, we better get home and shower so we aren't late for your church."

"Okay," Tess agreed. As they walked down the moun-

tain, volunteers walked up. They carefully lit each lumi-
naria, shining the way into Christmas Eve night.

Once home, Tess finished wrapping her presents.
Carefully crafting gold angels on a small square of white
paper, she wrapped Erin's angel box. She planned to
take it to church tonight, just in case. But first she
wanted to log into her prayer diary for just a minute.

Dear Jesus,

*Can you believe what Dad said on the mountain? He
actually knew that you were born in a desert, in Bethlehem. I'm a Christian, and I hadn't realized that. He
must have thought about this more than he lets on.
Thank you for helping my parents agree to go to
church with me. Please let him have a good time. Talk
with you later.*

Love, Tess

fifteen ✳

Christmas Surprise

Tuesday Evening, December 24

An hour or so after hiking, Tess ambled into the kitchen. "Could you please go out to the garage to get a new garbage bag for me?" her mother asked. They were hurrying to eat so they could drop Tess off for first service.

"Sure." Tess opened the garage door and reached for the bags. Maybe she should check to see if the doll-house was still there. The Navajo blanket lay limply in the corner. She lifted it up to see if the blanket still hid anything. Nothing. Her parents must have moved it to their closet until tomorrow morning. Could she seem happy when she opened it? Would it be lying to say she liked it? She really did like it; it was just a little too young for her. She might have liked it a few years ago. Oh, well. She grabbed the garbage bag and went back into the house.

"Here you go." She handed the bag to her mother.

"Thanks, honey. Say, Tess, what do people wear to your church? I mean, do they dress up? I want to make sure we wear something appropriate tonight." She put the finishing touches on the table and turned to face her daughter.

That sounded good. Tess hadn't really thought of it as her church but more like Erin's church. Of course it was hers. Plus, she enjoyed advising her mother on something.

"You can wear anything. Some people wear dresses, and some people wear jeans. It seems like everyone wears whatever he wants. I think I'll wear my jeans skirt."

"That sounds nice. Maybe I'll wear mine, too, and we'll dress up alike, like we did when you were little," her mom said. She ruffled Tess's hair.

Well, at least she was admitting Tess wasn't little anymore.

A bit later Mrs. Thomas dropped her off to work at first service and went home to pick up her husband and Tyler.

"Hi, Melissa. I'm here." Tess tied her nursery apron around her waist and picked up one of the toddlers who was crying.

Melissa waved at her but was too busy with several other children to say much. So many kids were in the nursery tonight. Tess was glad that a lot of people were in church. Maybe the parents of these kids were visitors like her parents would be. Her heart raced a bit at the thought. She hoped they would like it here.

"Let's sing 'Away in a Manger,'" she said, sitting on the floor with two kids on her lap. Several songs later things quieted down a bit and more helpers arrived. That allowed Tess and Melissa a chance to talk.

"Thanks for coming tonight. Your parents are visiting, right?"

"Yeah, they'll be here second service." Tess handed a card to Melissa. "I didn't know your address, so I just brought it."

"Thanks," Melissa said. "I have something for you, too." She dug a small box out of her apron pocket.

"Thanks," Tess said. "Should I open it now?"

"Sure, we have time."

Tess unwrapped a tiny beanbag baby.

"It's to remind you of us working in the nursery. I hope you don't think it's dumb," Melissa said, blushing a bit.

"No, I think it's cute. Look, it flops over when you set it down just like the real babies!" Tess giggled. Melissa giggled, too. Then they went back to work.

Soon it was time for second service, so Tess washed her hands, hung up her apron, and went to meet her parents in the sanctuary. What if they couldn't find a parking spot? What if Dad got irritated and it ruined Christmas? She didn't have much time to worry, because she spotted her family out of the corner of her eye.

"Hi, honey," her mother said. The three of them looked sort of stiff and uncomfortable. It was a new sensation for Tess, to feel comfortable when they didn't.

She determined to do everything she could to help them feel good about church.

"Come on, let's grab a seat," Tess said, leading the way. They found four open seats near the back and settled down. The sanctuary was abloom with red and white poinsettias, and an imposing Christmas tree stood front and center. The room's lights were dimmed, and as the service started, the choir came forward through the center aisle, singing carols. Everyone stood and read the words from the overhead screen. Tess glanced sideways at her parents, who seemed to be enjoying themselves. More relaxed now, she looked for Erin. She saw her sitting a few rows ahead with her parents and grandparents.

"I think I messed up the gift thing," Tess whispered to her mother during the announcements.

"Why?" her mom whispered back.

"Well, Melissa gave me something, and I only had a card for her."

"Don't worry." Her mother patted her hand. The sermon started, and Tess turned her attention to the pastor. What would she be telling her family if she fidgeted instead of listening? *Thank you, Lord,* she prayed silently, *for the best, best Christmas ever. The first Christmas that I know you are the Savior. I mean, I really understand why you were born. And thank you for Mom and Dad and Tyler and, of course, for our new baby. And Erin.* Her heart stuttered a little with the last thought.

In what seemed like only a few more minutes, the service was over. Her dad stood up to stretch. Tess didn't want to ask, but she must have looked at him expectantly, because he chuckled and hit her lightly on the shoulder. "It was fine, honey, as church goes. Now, are you ready to go home?"

"Yes." Tess turned to pick up her Bible. As she stood up, she saw Erin.

"Hi," Tess started, not knowing what else to say.

"Hi. Uh, can I talk to you for a second?" Erin asked, a pale pink flush lighting her face.

"Sure." Tess turned to her parents. "Can I meet you guys in the parking lot? It'll just take me a minute."

"Okay, but no longer. I'm beat!" her mom said, smiling at the two of them.

Erin and Tess sat down in the chairs of the rapidly emptying church. Erin fidgeted, then said, "I'm really sorry for being silly. I treated you badly, and I was wrong. Do you forgive me?" She sniffled a bit, and her eyes shone with unshed tears.

Tess reached her arm around Erin's shoulder. "Of course, Sis. Of course. I didn't mean to hurt your feelings. I really didn't care about talking to Scott except I knew you wanted him to hang around for a while. So I didn't want him to leave."

"I know. I guess I was just jealous because I didn't know what to say, and you always seem to know what to say. I wanted to make up with you at church on Sunday, but when you went to sit with Melissa and then stayed to talk with her afterward, I figured you were really mad at me and didn't want to talk at all. Which I would have understood totally since I was so rude. Then I lost my nerve and rushed out of Sunday school."

"No, no. Melissa just snagged me when I walked into the room so she could ask me if I'd help her out in the nursery tonight. I wanted to see you afterward, but you had gone. And you must be kidding about my knowing what to say all the time. I don't know what to say to half the world. Like your brother or the Coronado Club. Whenever I talk with any of them, I sound like a dork."

"Yeah, well, I was holding a grudge, and I'm sorry."

"Never mind. I knew we weren't going to break up our sisterhood over any old boy, no matter who it was."

"Right!" Erin agreed. "I was so glad to see your parents here tonight." Tess beamed back, and Erin continued, "Guess what? We each opened one present before church tonight, and I got—"

"The camp certificate!" Tess jumped in.

"Right! Now we can go together. It'll be such fun."

"Yeah, I guess so," Tess said. "I don't know though, with the dollhouse and all I don't think I'll be getting camp for Christmas."

"What about your craft money?"

"I'm sending that to the Christmas Angel program. Remember I told you about it?"

"Oh, yeah. All of it?" Erin asked.

"Well, fifty dollars, which is almost all of it," Tess answered.

"Why all of it? I mean, I think you can give part of it, and it would still be okay."

"I know. I thought so, too. It's just when I saw those kids at the mission yesterday, I don't know, I guess I wanted to send all of it." She changed the subject so she wouldn't have to think about not going to camp this summer. "I brought your present. Here." She slipped the box out of her sweater pocket and handed it to Erin. She was reluctant to give it to Erin, knowing she had thought their friendship would split up when she bought it. Now that they were together again, she didn't want their bracelets to be different.

"I didn't bring yours. I forgot. How about I save this until tomorrow, and I'll bring yours over in the morning, about ten o'clock. Then we can open them together," Erin said.

"Sure," Tess said. "I already have the best present—my sister back." She hugged Erin, and they stood up to leave.

"Till tomorrow?" Erin said, taking off her charm bracelet and holding it out to Tess to seal the deal.

Tess swallowed hard, knowing this would be the last time they switched identical bracelets, after Erin opened her Christmas present, that is. But Tess took off her bracelet and handed it over to Erin. "Till tomorrow," she agreed.

sixteen

Accidental Angel

Wednesday, December 25

Early Christmas morning Tess rolled out of bed and went to meet her family in the kitchen for breakfast. She glanced at the gifts in the family room, though, and changed her mind. "I'll be right there!" she called, stopping in the bathroom and closing the door.

Facing the mirror, she tried several forced smiles. One looked too surprised, like her eyebrows were pasted up. Her second try looked like a toothpaste commercial because her lips were peeled back and revealed too many teeth. Attempt number three looked totally fake. What was she going to do?

She sat down on the closed toilet lid and prayed, "Lord, I don't think I can pretend to smile when I open that dollhouse. Please help me to have real joy when I see my gift so I don't disappoint anyone but am not lying either." She hopped up and went out to the kitchen.

"I'm starving!" her mom said, watching Tess chop up

the French toast. It was the Thomas family tradition that every Christmas morning they dunked French toast, lightly dipped in egg batter, into a fondue of hot oil and then smothered it with maple syrup.

"I want the blue tong!" Tyler said, grabbing the long skewer with a blue knob.

"I don't care. I just don't want yellow. It has a chip in it," Tess answered.

"I'll take yellow," Dad said. "But that means I get to go first." He swirled a piece of bread until it was crispy and then popped it into his mouth. He put another on his fork, cooked it, and after dipping it into the maple syrup, handed it to his wife.

"Don't go getting all lovey-dovey on us now." Tyler plugged his nose. "This is a happy holiday, after all."

"Well, since you're so happy, why don't you open the first present?" Mr. Thomas said.

"Tyler, open mine first." Tess dug through the gifts and found the one she had wrapped for Tyler. On his package she had drawn a picture of Sherlock Holmes with his pipe and hat. Tyler took it from her and smiled.

"Great art! Thanks." First he slit the tape on all four sides, then carefully lifted the paper from around all four corners of the box. The process took him at least a minute, whereas it might have taken Tess ten seconds to rip off the whole deal.

"Gecko Grass! Thanks. Hercules will love it."

"Look," Tess said, "there's something else in there."

Tyler looked underneath the grass packaging and

found the Trapper, a net specially designed to help him catch quick crickets.

"Boffo, ol' girl!" Tyler walked over and gave her a hug. He was a good guy.

"Tess, do you want to go next?" her mom asked.

"No, why don't you guys open the one from Ty and me," Tess suggested, delaying a bit.

Tyler reached under the tree and pulled out the big box Tess had purchased two days earlier.

"Here, Jim, you open it." Molly Thomas handed over the box.

"Thanks, don't mind if I do." Just like Tyler, he carefully undid the tape and the wrappings on which Tess had traced her feet.

"My goodness, what a great idea!" Mrs. Thomas said as Tess's dad pulled the Sole Soother box from the wraps. "Just what my poor feet need right now."

"Mine too," Tess's dad said. "Especially after hiking! Let's give it a try after the gifts are all opened. This is the best gift you guys have ever bought us!"

Tess smiled, pleased to have picked out just the right gift.

"Get Tess's now," Tyler said.

Tess waited for her mother or father to go into the bedroom to bring out a big box since she didn't see any boxes large enough to be the dollhouse under the tree. To her surprise, her dad reached under the tree and pulled one out. Maybe she was getting two gifts. Or was this from her grandparents?

"To Tess. Love, Mom and Dad," she read and then

tore off the card and ripped through the paper. The box read "Authentic Tony Lama Riding Boots." Undoing the box as fast as she could, she pulled a pair of riding boots out of the box. "Oh, Mom and Dad, these are so beautiful!" The hand-tooled leather was worked into smooth suede on the inside but had tough support on the outside. Polished to a high shine, the boots had a turquoise horizon with shades of sunset. A tiny cactus wren design anchored the straps to the left and the right.

"Can I try them on?" she asked.

"Of course," her father said.

She still had on her pajamas, but her bare left foot slipped easily into the boot. When she tried to pull on the right boot, though, her foot crunched down on some paper. Quickly she pulled out her foot.

"What's this?" She reached into the boot and retrieved an envelope.

"Open it and see." Her mother's eyes danced with excitement.

Tess slit the envelope and read, "This is the deposit and confirmation for Tess Thomas. One week at the Lazy K Bar summer camp." She jumped up and down, one boot on and one boot off. "I can't believe it!"

"That's the trouble with girls. Hyper over everything," Tyler muttered, but Tess saw his smile.

"Why can't you believe it? You asked for the camp, and Dad thought it might be a fun surprise to give you the boots, too."

"I love it, I love it!" Tess ran over and kissed both her parents. "It's just, well . . ." She stopped.

"Just what, honey? Don't you want to go anymore?" Her mother looked confused.

"Well, what about the dollhouse?" Tess finally said.

"What dollhouse?" Her father looked puzzled.

"I say, ol' girl, you've really gone over the edge."

"I thought you guys were getting me a dollhouse."

"Why would you think that?" her mom asked.

"Well, when I went into the garage last week to look for boxes, I accidentally lifted up a blanket that was hiding a dollhouse. I knew it wasn't for Tyler so I just thought . . ."

Her mother and dad broke out laughing at the same time. "Oh, Tess," her mom said, "that dollhouse is for Christi Simons down the street. Her parents asked us to hide it for them so she wouldn't see it. They came and got it while you and Dad were hiking yesterday."

"Boy, do I feel dumb," Tess said. "But happy. I am so surprised!"

"Then you are *really* going to be surprised next month at your birthday," Tyler said, then clapped his hand over his mouth.

"Tyler!" his mom and dad said at once.

"Sorry, ol' girl. Almost made a bloomer of a mistake."

"What do you mean?" Tess was curious. What surprise could they have planned for her birthday?

"You'll just have to wait and see," her mom said. "Now, let's get back to Christmas."

Just then the doorbell rang. "That must be Erin. I'll get it," Tess said, hobbling to the door in her pajamas, with one boot on.

"But, Tess . . . ," Her mother tried to warn her of her attire, but Tess wasn't listening.

"Hi!" Tess said as a fully dressed Erin appeared at the door. "Guess what?"

"Gee, sorry I'm early." Erin looked Tess up and down.

Tess realized she was in her jammies with a peg leg boot. She looked at Erin. Worse yet, she looked beyond Erin, where the whole Janssen family, including Tom, sat in the car, staring at her.

"Oh, no!" she said. "Come in." Erin scooted in, and Tess shut the door behind her. "I just took a first-class trip to embarrassment land," Tess said. "But guess what!"

Erin looked down at her boot. "You got boots?"

"Yes, and camp!" Tess exclaimed. "I really messed up on the dollhouse. It wasn't for me, after all, but for a neighbor. I got Tony Lama boots and the deposit to camp!"

"Great!" Erin jumped up and down with excitement, and Tess did, too.

"We'd better exchange gifts, 'cause we're supposed to be at my grandparents' house in a few minutes," Erin said as she settled down and handed Tess a small box.

"Open mine first," Tess said.

Erin opened the gift wrapped in handmade paper and smiled broadly.

"Well, do you like it? I bought it because it reminded me of the cookies we baked."

"Open mine," Erin said.

Tess ripped into the package. She gasped when she

saw what it was. "I can't believe it! We bought the same thing!" They broke out in giggles.

"I was so sad because our bracelets wouldn't match anymore," Tess said. "But I was wrong!"

"I bought yours at the mall by my grandma's. It's especially true now that I know you're giving away most of your craft-fair money, you angel," Erin giggled.

"Well, it's not like I can take credit for it. I didn't plan to do that, and I had to think about it," Tess reminded her.

"But you could have sent in five dollars. So you're still an angel. An accidental angel!" They laughed again, and after affixing the new charms, they switched bracelets.

"Here's to the best Christmas yet, the first of one hundred as Secret Sisters," Erin offered, and Tess agreed. It was her best Christmas ever.

Have More Fun!!

Visit the official website at:
www.secretsisters.com

There are lots of activities, exciting contests, and a chance for YOU to tell me what you'd like to see in future Secret Sisters books! AND—be the first to know when the next Secret Sisters book will be at your bookstore by signing up for the instant e-mail update list. See you there today!

Stained-Glass Christmas Angels

Make these sweet treats with your Secret Sis, then invite some other friends over for a Christmas Cookie Exchange!

For 4 dozen cookies you'll need:

2 ¾ cups flour
½ teaspoon baking powder
½ teaspoon salt
⅔ cup sugar
1 cup butter, softened
One large egg, lightly beaten
1 ½ teaspoons vanilla
Hard candy or Sour Balls

In a large mixing bowl cream together sugar and butter until fluffy. Add the egg and vanilla, and beat until blended. With the beater running at low speed, mix in the flour, baking powder, and salt. Mix just until the dough can be shaped into a ball.

Wrap dough in waxed paper, and set in refrigerator for ½ hour.

Separate the candies by color, and place each color in a plastic bag. Close bag, and smash the bag with a meat tenderizer until candy is broken into small pieces. (Or have your mom crush the candy in a food processor instead.)

With rolling pin, roll dough on a lightly floured surface until the dough is 1/4-inch thick.

Cut out cookies using a 3-inch angel-shaped cookie cutter. Place the cookies on lightly greased aluminum-foil-covered cookie sheets. Using a knife, cut out the inside of each angel wing, remove the dough from that section, and fill with crushed candy.

Bake at 350 degrees for 8-10 minutes until the cookies are lightly browned and the candy has melted.

Allow the cookies to cool completely on the sheets, then carefully peel off the foil.

Store in airtight container between sheets of waxed paper at room temperature. Keeps for several weeks.

How can we keep your interest alive? Solve this puzzle for clues to Book Five!

Across

1 If you are separated from someone you love, you're...
5 Opposite of succeed
7 Another name for a slumber party
10 Where to mark your day-to-days
11 The kind of friends Tess and Erin are
13 A sport with 10 pins and a heavy ball
14 You fix it every morning and cut it every month
15 Bars and beams, sometimes crushed dreams
18 Opposite of somebody

Down

2 Book in the Bible just before Proverbs
3 How old is Tess this birthday?
4 Decisions
6 A contest testing skill or ability
8 The game, Truth, _____, Double Dare, Promise or Repeat
9 The Bible says it sets you free
11 Infant
12 Tests and practices to determine if you are qualified for a team
16 Opposite of reject
17 What you do when you're anxious

Look for the Other Titles in
Sandra Byrd's Secret Sisters Series!
Available at your local Christian bookstore

Available Now:

#1 *Heart to Heart:* When the exclusive Coronado Club invites Tess Thomas to join, she thinks she'll do anything to belong—until she finds out just how much is required.

#2 *Twenty-One Ponies:* There are plenty of surprises—and problems—in store for Tess. But a Native American tale teaches her just how much God loves her.

#3 *Star Light:* Tess's mother becomes seriously ill, and Tess's new faith is tested. Can she trust God with the big things as well as the small?

#4 *Accidental Angel:* Tess and Erin have great plans for their craft-fair earnings. But after their first big fight will they still want to spend it together? And how does Tess become the "accidental" angel?

✳

Available September 1998:

#5 *Double Dare:* A game of "truth o   leaves Tess feel-
ing like she doesn't measure up. Will   g the gymnastics
team prove she can excel?

#6 *War Paint:* Tess must choose between running for Miss Coronado and entering the school mural painting contest with Erin. There are big opportunities—and a big blowout with the Coronado Club.

✳

Available May 1999:

#7 *Holiday Hero:* This could be the best Spring Break ever—or the worst. Tess's brother, Tyler, is saved from disaster, but can the sisters rescue themselves from even bigger problems?

#8 *Petal Power:* Ms. Martinez is the most beautiful bride in the world, and the sisters are there to help her get married. When trouble strikes her honeymoon plans, Tess and Erin must find a way to help save them.

The Top Secret Sister Handbook: 101 Cool Ideas for You and Your Secret Sister! It's fun to read about Tess and Erin and just as fun to do things with your own Secret Sister! This book is jam-packed with great things for you to do together all year long.